TALES OF THE JUMBEE
AND OTHER WONDERS OF THE WEST INDIES

TALES OF THE JUMBEE
AND OTHER WONDERS OF THE WEST INDIES

Henry S. Whitehead

WILDSIDE PRESS

TALES OF THE JUMBEE
AND OTHER WONDERS OF THE WEST INDIES

"Jumbee" originally appeared in *Weird Tales* (1926). "The Shadows" originally appeared in *Weird Tales* (1927). "Cassius" originally appeared in *Strange Tales* (1931). "Black Tancrède" originally appeared in *Weird Tales* (1929). "Sweet Grass" originally appeared in *Weird Tales* (1929). "Mrs. Lorriquer" originally appeared in *Weird Tales* (1932). "The Passing of a God" originally appeared in *Weird Tales* (1931). "Hill Drums" originally appeared in *Weird Tales* (1931).

CONTENTS

JUMBEE

MR. GRANVILLE LEE, a Virginian of Virginians, coming out of the World War with a lung wasted and scorched by mustard gas, was recommended by his physician to spend a winter in the spice-and-balm climate of the Lesser Antilles—the lower islands of the West Indian archipelago. He chose one of the American islands, St. Croix, the old Santa Cruz—Island of the Holy Cross—named by Columbus himself on his second voyage; once famous for its rum.

It was to Jaffray Da Silva that Mr. Lee at last turned for definite information about the local magic; information which, after a two months' residence, accompanied with marked improvement in his general health, he had come to regard as imperative, from the whetting glimpses he had received of its persistence on the island.

Contact with local customs, too, had sufficiently blunted his inherited sensibilities, to make him almost comfortable, as he sat with Mr. Da Silva on the cool gallery of that gentleman's beautiful house, in the shade of forty years' growth of bougainvillea, on a certain afternoon. It was the restful gossipy period between five o'clock and dinnertime. A glass jug of foaming rum-swizzle stood on the table between them.

"But, tell me, Mr. Da Silva," he urged, as he absorbed his second glass of the cooling, mild drink, "have you ever, actually, been confronted with a 'Jumbee'?—ever really seen one? You say, quite frankly, that you believe in them!"

This was not the first question about Jumbees that Mr. Lee had asked. He had consulted planters; he had spoken of the matter of Jumbees with courteous, intelligent, colored storekeepers about the town, and even in Christiansted, St. Croix's other and larger town on the north side of the island. He had even mentioned the matter to one or two coal-black sugar-field laborers; for he had been on the island just long enough to begin to understand—a little—the weird jargon of speech which Lafcadio Hearn, when he visited St. Croix many years before, had not recognized as "English!"

There had been marked differences in what he had been told. The planters and storekeepers had smiled, though with varying degrees of intensity, and had replied that the Danes had invented Jumbees, to keep their estate-laborers indoors after nightfall, thus ensuring a proper night's sleep for them, and minimizing the depredations upon growing crops. The laborers whom he had asked, had rolled their eyes somewhat, but, it being broad daylight at the time of the enquiries, they had broken their impassive gravity with smiles, and sought to impress Mr. Lee with their lofty contempt for the beliefs of their fellow blacks, and with queerly-phrased assurances that Jumbee is a figment of the imagination.

Nevertheless, Mr. Lee was not satisfied. There was something here that he seemed to be missing—something extremely interesting, too, it appeared to him; something very different from "Bre'r Rabbit" and similar tales of his own remembered childhood in Virginia.

Once, too, he had been reading a book about Martinique and Guadeloupe, those ancient jewels of France's crown, and he had not read far before he met the word "Zombi." After that, he knew, at least, that the Danes had not "invented" the Jumbee. He heard, though vaguely, of the laborer's belief that Sven Garik, who had long ago gone back to his home in Sweden, and Carrity, one of the smaller planters now on the island, were "wolves!" Lycanthropy, animal-metamorphosis, it appeared, formed part of this strange texture of local belief.

Mr. Jaffray Da Silva was one-eighth African. He was, therefore, by island usage, "colored," which is as different from being "black" in the West Indies as anything that can be imagined. Mr. Da Silva had been educated in the continental European manner. In his every word and action, he reflected the faultless courtesy of his European forbears. By every right and custom of West Indian society, Mr. Da Silva was a colored gentleman, whose social status was as clear-cut and definite as a cameo.

These islands are largely populated by persons like Mr. Da Silva. Despite the difference in their status from what it would be in North America, in the islands it has its advantages—among them that of logic. To the West Indian mind, a man whose heredity is seven-eighths derived from gentry, as like as not with authentic coats-of^p arms, is entitled to be treated accordingly. That is why Mr. Da Silva's many clerks, and everybody else who knew him, treated him with deference, addressed him as "sir," and doffed their hats in continental fashion when meeting; salutes which, of course, Mr. Da Silva invariably returned, even to the humblest, which is one of the marks of a gentleman anywhere.

Jaffray Da Silva shifted one thin leg, draped in spotless white drill, over the other, and lighted a fresh cigarette.

"Even my friends smile at me, Mr. Lee," he replied, with a tolerant smile, which lightened for an instant his melancholy, ivory-white countenance. "They laugh at me more or less because I admit I believe in Jumbees. It is possible that everybody with even a small amount of African blood possesses that streak of belief in magic and the like. I seem, though, to have a peculiar aptitude for it! It is a matter of *experience,* with me, sir, and my friends are free to smile at me if they wish. Most of them—well, they do not admit their beliefs as freely as I, perhaps!"

Mr. Lee took another sip of the cold swizzle. He had heard how difficult it was to get Jaffray Da Silva to speak of his "experiences," and he suspected that under his host's even courtesy lay that austere pride which resents anything like ridicule, despite that tolerant smile.

"Please proceed, sir," urged Mr. Lee, and was quite unconscious that he had just used a word which, in his native South, is reserved for gentlemen of pure Caucasian blood.

"When I was a young man," began Mr. Da Silva, "about 1894, there was a friend of mine named Hilmar Iversen, a Dane, who lived here in the town, up near the Moravian Church on what the people call 'Foun'-Out Hill.' Iversen had a position under the government, a clerk's job, and his office was in the Fort. On his way home he used to stop here almost every afternoon for a swizzle and a chat. We were great friends, close friends. He was then a man a little past fifty, a butter-tub of a fellow, very stout, and, like many of that build, he suffered from heart attacks.

"One night a boy came here for me. It was eleven o'clock, and I was just arranging the mosquito-net on my bed, ready to turn in. The servants had all gone home, so I went to the door myself, in shirt and trousers, and carrying a lamp, to see what was wanted—or, rather, I knew perfectly well what it was—a messenger to tell me Iversen was dead!"

Mr. Lee suddenly sat bolt-upright.

"How could you know that?" he enquired, his eyes wide.

Mr. Da Silva threw away the remains of his cigarette.

"I sometimes know things like that," he answered, slowly. "In this case, Iversen and I had been close friends for years. He and I had talked about magic and that sort of thing a great deal, occult powers, manifestations—that sort of thing. It is a very general topic here, as you may have seen. You would hear more of it if you continued to live here and settled into the ways of the island. In fact, Mr. Lee, Iversen and I had made a compact together. The one of us who 'went out' first, was to try to warn the other of it. You see, Mr. Lee, I had received Iversen's warning less than an hour before.

"I had been sitting out here on the gallery until ten o'clock or so. I was in that very chair you are occupying. Iversen had been having a heart attack. I had been to see him that afternoon. He looked just as he always did when he was recovering from an attack. In fact he intended to return to his office the following morning. Neither of us, I am sure, had given a thought to the possibility of a sudden sinking spell. We had not even referred to our agreement.

"Well, it was about ten, as I've said, when all of a sudden I heard Iversen coming along through the yard below there, toward the house along that gravel path. He had, apparently, come through the gate from the Kongensgade—the King Street, as they call it nowadays—and I could hear his heavy step on the gravel very plainly. He had a slight limp. 'Heavy-crunch—light crunch; plod-plod—plod-plod'; old Iversen to the life; there was no mistaking his step. There was no moon that night. The half of a waning moon was due to show itself an hour and a half later, but just then it was virtually pitch-black down there in the garden.

"I got up out of my chair and walked over to the top of the steps. To tell you the truth, Mr. Lee, I rather suspected—I have a kind of aptitude for that sort of thing—that it was not Iversen himself; how shall I express it? I had the idea from somewhere inside me, that it was Iversen trying to keep our agreement. My instinct assured me that he had just died. I can not tell you how I knew it, but such was the case, Mr. Lee.

"So I waited, over there just behind you, at the top of the steps. The footfalls came along steadily. At the foot of the steps, out of the shadow of the hibiscus bushes, it was a trifle less black than farther down the path. There was a faint illumination, too, from a lamp inside the house. I knew that if it were Iversen, himself, I should be able to see him when the footsteps passed out of the deep shadow of the bushes. I did not speak.

"The footfalls came along toward that point, and passed it. I strained my eyes through the gloom, and I could see nothing. Then I knew, Mr. Lee, that Iversen had died, and that he was keeping his agreement.

"I came back here and sat down in my chair, and waited. The footfalls began to come up the steps. They came along the floor of the gallery, straight toward me. They stopped here, Mr. Lee, just beside me. I could *feel* Iversen standing here, Mr. Lee." Mr. Da Silva pointed to the floor with his slim, rather elegant hand.

"Suddenly, in the dead quiet, I could feel my hair stand up all over my scalp, straight and stiff. The chills started to run down my back, and up again, Mr. Lee. I shook like a man with the ague, sitting here in my chair.

"I said: 'Iversen, I understand! Iversen, I'm afraid!' My teeth were chattering like castanets, Mr. Lee. I said: 'Iversen, please go! You have kept the agreement. I am sorry I am afraid, Iversen. The flesh is weak! I am not afraid of you, Iversen, old friend. But you will understand, man! It's not ordinary fear. My intellect is all right, Iversen, but I'm badly panic-stricken, so please go, my friend.'

"There had been silence, Mr. Lee, as I said, before I began to speak to Iversen, for the footsteps had stopped here beside me. But when I said that, and asked my friend to go, I could feel that he went at once, and I knew that he had understood how I meant it! It was, suddenly, Mr. Lee, as though there bad never been any footsteps, if you see what I mean. It is hard to put into words. I daresay, if I had been one of the laborers, I should have been halfway to Christiansted through the estates, Mr. Lee, but I was not so frightened that I could not stand my ground.

"After I had recovered myself a little, and my scalp had ceased its prickling, and the chills were no longer running up and down my spine, I rose, and I felt extremely weary, Mr. Lee. It had been exhausting. I came into the house and drank a large tot of French brandy, and then I felt better, more like myself. I took my hurricane-lantern and lighted it, and stepped down the path toward the gate leading to the Kongensgade. There was one thing I wished to see down there at the end of the garden. I wanted to see if the gate was fastened, Mr. Lee. It was. That huge iron staple that you noticed, was in place. It has been used to fasten that old gate since some time in the Eighteenth Century, I imagine. I had not supposed anyone had opened the gate, Mr. Lee, but now I knew. There were no footprints in the gravel, Mr. Lee. I looked, carefully. The marks of the bush-broom where the house-boy had swept the path on his way back from closing the gate were undisturbed, Mr. Lee.

"I was satisfied, and no longer, even a little frightened. I came back here and sat down, and thought about my long friendship with old Iversen. I felt very sad to know that I should not see him again alive. He would never stop here again afternoons for a swizzle and a chat. About 11 o'clock I went inside the house and was preparing for bed when the rapping came at the front door. You see, Mr. Lee, I knew at once what it would mean.

"I went to the door, in shirt and trousers and stocking feet, carrying a lamp. We did not have electric light in those days. At the door stood Iversen's house-boy, a young fellow about eighteen. He was half-asleep, and very much upset. He 'cut his eyes' at me, and said nothing.

"'What is it, mon?' I asked the boy.

"'Mistress Iversen send ax yo' sir, please come to de house. Mr. Iversen die, sir.'

"'What time Mr. Iversen die, mon—you hear?'

"'I ain' able to say what o'clock, sir. Mistress Iversen come wake me where I sleep in a room in the yard, sir, an' sen' me please cahl you,—I t'ink he die aboht an hour ago, sir.'

"I put on my shoes again, and the rest of my clothes, and picked up a St. Kitts supplejack—I'll get you one; it's one of those limber, grapevine walking sticks, a handy thing on a dark night—and started with the boy for Iversen's house.

"When we had arrived almost at the Moravian Church, I saw something ahead, near the roadside. It was then about eleven-fifteen, and the streets were deserted. What I saw made me curious to test something. I paused, and told the boy to run on ahead and tell Mrs. Iversen I would be there shortly. The boy started to trot ahead. He was pure black, Mr. Lee, but he went past what I saw without noticing it. He swerved a little away from it, and I think, perhaps, he slightly quickened his pace just at that point, but that was all."

"What did you see?" asked Mr. Lee, interrupting. He spoke a trifle breathlessly. His left lung was, as yet, far from being healed.

"The 'Hanging Jumbee,'" replied Mr. Da Silva, in his usual tones.

"Yes! There at the side of the road were three Jumbees. There's a reference to that in *The History of Stewart Mc-Cann.* Perhaps you've run across that, eh?"

Mr. Lee nodded, and Mr. Da Silva quoted:

> "There they hung. though no ladder's rung
> Supported their dangling feet.

"And there's another line in *The History,*" he continued, smiling, "which describes a typical group of Hanging Jumbee:

> "Maiden, man-child, and shrew.

"Well, there were the usual three Jumbees, apparently hanging in the air. It wasn't very light, but I could make out a boy of about twelve, a young girl, and a shriveled old woman—what the author of *The History of Stewart McCann* meant by the word 'shrew.' He told me himself, by the way, Mr. Lee, that he had put feet on his Jumbees mostly for the sake of a convenient rime—poetic license! The Hanging Jumbee have no feet. It is one of their peculiarities. Their legs stop at the ankles. They have abnormally long, thin legs—African legs. They are always black, you know. Their feet—if they have them—are always hidden in a kind of mist that lies along the ground wherever one sees them. They shift and 'weave,' as a full-blooded African does—standing on one foot and resting the other—you've noticed that, of course—or scratching the supporting ankle with the toes of the other foot. They do not swing in the sense that they seem to be swung on a rope—that is not what it means; they do not twirl about. But they do—always—face the oncomer. . . .

"I walked on, slowly, and passed them; and they kept their faces to me as they always do. I'm used to that. . . .

"I went up the steps of the house to the front gallery, and found Mrs. Iversen waiting for me. Her sister was with her, too. I remained sitting with them for the best part of an hour. Then two old black women who had been sent for, into the country, arrived. These were two old women who were accustomed to prepare the dead for burial. Then I persuaded the ladies to retire, and started to come home myself.

"it was a little past midnight, perhaps twelve-fifteen. I picked out my own hat from two or three of poor old Iversen's that were hanging on the rack, took my supplejack, and stepped out of the door onto the little stone gallery at the head of the steps.

"There are about twelve or thirteen steps from the gallery down to the street As I started down them I noticed a third old black woman sitting all huddled together on the bottom step, with her back to me. I thought at once that this must be some old crone who lived with the other two—the preparers of the dead. I imagined that she had been afraid to remain alone in their cabin, and so had accompanied them into the town-they are like children, you know, in some ways—and that, feeling too humble to come into the house, she had sat down to wait on the step and had fallen asleep. You've heard their proverbs, have you not? There's one that exactly fits this situation that I had imagined: 'Cockroach no wear crockin' boot when he creep in fowl-house!' It means: 'Be very reserved when in the presence of your betters!' Quaint, rather! The poor souls!

"I started to walk down the steps toward the old woman. That scant halfmoon had come up into the sky while I had been sitting with the ladies, and by its light everything was fairly sharply defined. I could see that old woman as plainly as I can see you now, Mr. Lee. In fact, I was looking directly at the poor old creature as I came, down the steps, and fumbling in my pocket for a few coppers for her—for tobacco and sugar, as they say! I was wondering, indeed, why she was not by this time on her feet and making one of their queer little bobbing bows—'cockroach bow to fowl,' as they might say! It seemed this old woman must have fallen into a very deep sleep, for she bad not moved at all, although ordinarily she would have heard me, for the night was deathly still, and their hearing is extraordinarily acute, like a cat's, or a dog's. I remember that the fragrance from Mrs. Iversen's tuberoses, in pots on the gallery railing, was pouring out in a stream that night, 'making a greeting for the moon!' It was almost overpowering.

"Just as I was putting my foot on the fifth step, there came a tiny little puff of fresh breeze from somewhere in the hills behind Iversen's house. It rustled the dry fronds of a palm-tree that was growing beside the steps. I turned my head in that direction for an instant.

"Mr. Lee, when I looked back; down the steps, after what must have been a fifth of a second's inattention, that little old black woman who had been huddled up there on the lowest step, apparently sound asleep, was gone. She had vanished utterly—and, Mr. Lee, a little white dog, about the size of a French poodle, was bounding up the steps toward me. With every bound, a step at a leap, the dog increased in size. It seemed to swell out there before my very eyes.

"Then I was, really, frightened—thoroughly, utterly frightened. I knew if that 'animal' so much as touched me, it meant death, Mr. Lee— absolute, certain death. The little old woman was a 'sheen'—*chien,* of course. You know of lycanthropy—wolf-change—of course. Well, this was one of our varieties of it. I do not know what it would be called, I'm sure. 'Canicanthropy,' perhaps. I don't know, but something—something first-cousin-once-removed from lycanthropy, and on the downward scale, Mr. Lee. The old woman was a were-dog!

"Of course, I had no time to think, only to use my instinct. I swung my supplejack with all my might and brought it down squarely on that beast's head. It was only a step below me, then, and I could see the faint moonlight sparkle on the slaver about its mouth. It was then, it seemed to me, about the size of a medium-sized dog—nearly wolf-size, Mr. Lee, and a kind of deathly white. I was desperate, and the force with which I struck caused me to lose my balance. I did not fall, but it required a moment or two for me to regain my equilibrium. When I felt my feet firm under me again, I looked about, frantically, on all sides, for the 'dog.' But it, too, Mr. Lee, like the old woman, had quite disappeared. I looked all about, you may well imagine, after that experience, in the clear, thin moonlight. For yards about the foot of the steps, there was no place—not even a small nook—where either the 'dog' or the old woman could have been concealed. Neither was on the gallery, which was only a few feet square, a mere landing.

"But there came to my ears, sharpened by that night's experiences, from far out among the plantations at the rear of Iversen's house, the pad-pad of naked feet. Someone—something—was running, desperately, off in the direction of the center of the island, back into the hills, into the deep 'bush.'

"Then, behind me, out of the house onto the gallery rushed the two old women who had been preparing Iversen's body for its burial. They were enormously excited, and they shouted at me unintelligibly. I will have to render their words for you.

"'O, de Good Gahd protec' you, Marster Jaffray, sir—de Joombie, de Joombie! De 'Sheen,' Marster Jaffray! He go, sir?'

"I reassured the poor old souls, and went back home."

Mr. Da Silva fell abruptly silent. He slowly shifted his position in his chair, and reached for, and lighted, a fresh cigarette.

Mr. Lee was absolutely silent. He did not move. Mr. Da Silva resumed, deliberately, after obtaining a light.

"You see, Mr. Lee, the West Indies are different from any other place in the world, I verily believe, sir. I've said so, anyhow, many a time, although I have never been out of the islands except when I was a young man, to Copenhagen. I've told you, exactly, what happened that particular night."

Mr. Lee heaved a sigh.

"Thank you, Mr. Da Silva, very much indeed, sir," said he, thoughtfully, and made as though to rise. His service wrist-watch indicated 8 o'clock.

"Let us have a fresh swizzel, at least, before you go," suggested Mr. Da Silva. "We have a saying here in the island, that 'a man can't travel on one leg!' Perhaps you've heard it already."

"I have," said Mr. Lee.

"Knud, Knud! You hear, mon? Knud—tell Charlotte to mash up another bal' of ice—you hear? Quickly now," commanded Mr. Da Silva.

THE SHADOWS
THE SHADOWS

I DID not begin to see the shadows until I had lived in Old Morris' house for more than a week. Old Morris, dead and gone these many years, had been the scion of a still earlier Irish settler in Santa Cruz, of a family which had come into the island when the Danes, failing to colonize its rich acres, had opened it, in the middle of the Eighteenth Century, to colonists; and younger sons of Irish, Scottish, and English gentry had taken up sugar estates and commenced that baronial life which lasted for a century and which declined after the abolition of slavery and the German bounty on beet sugar had started the long process of West Indian commercial decadence. Mr. Morris' youth had been spent in the French islands.

The shadows were at first so vague that I attributed them wholly to the slight weakness which began to affect my eyes in early childhood, and which, while never materially interfering with the enjoyment of life in general, had necessitated the use of glasses when I used my eyes to read or write. My first experience of them was about one o'clock in the morning. I had been at a "Gentlemen's Party" at Hacker's house, "Emerald," as some poetic-minded ancestor of Hacker's had named the family estate three miles out of Christiansted, the northerly town, built on the site of the ancient abandoned French town of Bassin.

I had come home from the party and was undressing in my bedroom, which is one of two rooms on the westerly side of the house which stands at the edge of the old "Sunday Market." These two bedrooms open on the market-place, and I had chosen them, rather than the more airy rooms on the other side, because of the space outside. I like to look out on trees in the early mornings, whenever possible, and the ancient market-place is overshadowed with the foliage of hundred-year-old mahogany trees, and a few gnarled "otaheites" and Chinese-bean trees.

I had nearly finished undressing, had noted that my servant had let down and properly fastened the mosquito netting, and had stepped into the other bedroom to open the jalousies so that I might get as much of the night-breeze as possible circulating through the house. I was coming back through the doorway between the two bedrooms, and taking off my dressing gown, at the moment, when the first faint perception of what I have called "the shadows" made itself apparent. It was very dark, just after switching off the electric light in that front bedroom. I had, in fact, to feel for the doorway. In this I experienced some difficulty, and my eyes had not fully adjusted themselves to the thin starlight seeping in through the slanted jalousies of my own room when I passed through the doorway and groped my way toward the great mahogany four-poster in which I was about to lie down for my belated rest.

I saw the nearest post looming before me, closer than I had expected. Putting out my hand, I grasped—nothing. I winked in some surprize, and peered through the slightly increasing light, as my eyes adjusted themselves to the sudden change. Yes, surely,—there was the corner of the bedstead just in front of my face! By now my eyes were sufficiently attuned to the amount of light from outside to see a little plainer. I was puzzled. The bed was not where I had supposed it to be. What could have happened? That the servants should have moved my bed without orders to do so was incredible. Besides, I had undressed, in full electric light in that room, not more than a few minutes ago, and then the bed was standing exactly where it had been since I had had it moved into that room a week before. I kicked gently, before me with a slippered foot, against the place where that bedpost appeared to be standing—and my foot met no resistance.

I stepped over to the light in my own room. and snapped the button. In the sudden glare, everything readjusted itself to normal. There stood my bed, and here in their accustomed places about the room were ranged the chairs, the polished wardrobe (we do not use cupboards in the West India Islands), the mahogany dressing table,—even my clothes which I had hung over a chair where Albertina my servant would find them in the morning and put them (they were of white drill) into the soiled-clothes bag in the morning.

I shook my head. Light and shadow in these islands seem, somehow, different from what they are like at home in the United States! The tricks they play are different tricks, somehow.

I snapped off the light again, and in the ensuing dead blackness, I crawled in under the loose edge of the mosquito netting, tucked it along under the edge of the mattress on that side, adjusted my pil!ows and the sheets, and settled myself for a good sleep. Even to a moderate man, these gentlemen's parties are rather wearing sometimes. They invariably last too long. I closed my eyes and was asleep before I could have put these last ideas into words.

In the morning the recollection Of the experience with the bed-being-in-the-wrong-place was gone. I jumped out of bed and into my shower bath at half-past six, for I had promised O'Brien, captain of the U. S. Marines, to go out with him to the rifle range at La Grande Princesse that morning and look over the butts with him. I like O'Brien, and I am not uninterested in the efficiency of Uncle Sam's Marines, but my chief objective was to watch the pelicans. Out there on the glorious

the outward and visible sign of something which animates it. All normal human beings, it seems to me, are sacramentalists!

I was, for this reason, able to thing clearly about the phenomenon. My mind was not clouded and bemused with fear, and its known physiological effects. I can, quite easily, record what I "saw" in the course of the next few days. The bed was clearer to my vision and apprehension than it had been. It seemed to have grown in visibility; in a kind of substantialness, if there is such a word! It appeared more *material* than it had before, less shadowy.

I looked about the room and saw other furniture: a huge, old-fashioned mahogany bureau with men's heads carved on the knuckles of the front legs, Danish fashion. There is precisely such carving on pieces in the museum in Copenhagen, they tell me, those who have seen my drawing of it. I was actually able to do that, and had completed a kind of plan-picture of the room, putting in all the shadow-furniture, and leaving my own, actual furniture out. Thank the God in whom I devoutly believe,—and know to be more powerful than the Powers of Evil,—I was able to finish that rather elaborate drawing before. . . Well, I must not "run ahead of my story."

That night when I was ready to retire, and had once more opened up the jalousies of the front bedroom, and had switched off the light, I looked, naturally enough under the circumstances, for the outlines of that ghostly furniture. They were much clearer now. I studied them with a certain sense of almost "scientific" detachment. It was, even then, apparent to me that no weakness of the strange complexity which is the human eye could reasonably account for the presence of a well-defined set of mahogany furniture in a room already furnished with real furniture! But I was by now sufficiently accustomed to it to be able to examine it all without that always-disturbing element of fear,—strangeness. I looked at the bedstead and the "roll-back" chairs, and the great bureau, and a ghostly, huge, and quaintly carved wardrobe, studying their outlines, noting their relative positions. It was on that occasion that it occurred to me that it would be of interest to make some kind of drawing of them. I looked the harder after that, fixing the details and the relations of them all in my mind, and then I went into the hall and got some paper and a pencil and set to work.

It was hard work, this of reproducing something which I was well aware was some kind of an "apparition," especially after looking at the furniture in the dark bedroom, switching on the light in another room and then trying to reproduce. I could not, of course, make a direct comparison. I mean it was impossible to look at my drawing and then look at the furniture. There was always a necessary interval between the two processes. I persisted through several evenings, and even for a couple of evenings fell into the custom of going into my bedroom in the evening's darkness, looking at what was there, and then attempting to reproduce it. After five or six days, I had a fair plan, in considerable detail, of the arrangement of this strange furniture in my bedroom,-a plan or drawing which would be recognizable if there were anyone now alive who remembered such arrangement of such furniture. It will be apparent that a story had been growing up in my mind, or, at least, that I had come to some kind of conviction that what I "saw" was a reproduction of something that had once existed in that same detail and that precise order!

On the seventh night, there came an interruption.

I had, by that time, finished my work, pretty well. I had drawn the room as it would have looked with that furniture in it, and had gone over the whole with India ink, very carefully. As a drawing, the thing was finished, so far as my indifferent skill as a draftsman would permit.

That seventh evening, I was looking over the appearance of the room, such qualms as the eeriness of the situation might have otherwise produced reduced to next-to-nothing partly by my interest, in part by having become accustomed to it all. I was making, this evening, as careful a comparison as possible between my remembered work on paper and the detailed appearance of the room. By now, the furniture stood out clearly, in a kind of light of its own which I can roughly compare only to "phosphorescence." It was not, quite, that. But that will serve, lame as it is, and trite perhaps, to indicate what I mean. I suppose the appearance of the room was something like what a cat "sees" when she arches her back,—as Algernon Blackwood has pointed out, in *John Silence,*—and rubs against the imaginary legs of some personage entirely invisible to the man in the armchair who idly wonders what has taken possession of his house-pet.

I was, as I say, studying the detail. I could not find that I had left out anything salient. The detail was, too, quite clear now. There were no blurred outlines as there had been on the first few nights. My own, material furniture had, so to speak, sunk back into invisibility, which was sensible enough, seeing that I had put the room in as nearly perfect darkness as I could, and there was no moon to interfere, those nights.

I had run my eyes all around it, up and down the twisted legs of the great bureau, along the carved ornamentation of the top of the wardrobe, along the lines of the chairs, and come back to the bed. It was at this point of my checking-up that I got what I must describe as the first "shock" of the entire experience.

Something moved, beside the bed.

I peered, carefully, straining my eyes to catch what it might be. It had been something bulky, a slow-moving object, on the far side of the bed, blurred, somewhat, just as the original outlines had been blurred in the beginning of my week's experience. The now strong and clear outlines of the bed, and what I might describe as its ethereal substance, stood between me and it. Besides, the vision of the slow-moving mass was further obscured by a ghostly mosquito-net, which had been one of the last of the details to come into the scope of my strange night-vision.

Those folds of the mosquito-netting moved,—waved, before my eyes.

Someone, it might almost be imagined, was getting into that bed!

I sat, petrified. This was a bit too much for me. I could feel the little chills run up and down my spine. My scalp prickled. I put my hands on my knees, and pressed hard. I drew several deep breaths. "All-overish" is an old New England expression, once much used by spinsters, I believe, resident in that intellectual section of the United States. Whatever the precise connotation of the term, that was way I felt. I could feel the reactive sensation, I mean, of that particular portion of the whole experience, in every part of my being,—body, mind, and soul! It was,—paralyzing. I reached up a hand that was trembling violently,—I could barely control it, and the fingers, when they touched the hard-rubber button, felt numb,—and switched on the bedroom light, and spent the next ten minutes recovering.

That night, when I came to retire, I dreaded,—actually dreaded,—what might come to my vision when I snapped off the light. This, however, I managed to reason out with myself. I used several arguments—nothing had so far occurred to annoy or injure me; if this were to be a cumulative experience, if something were to be "revealed" to me by this deliberate process of slow materialization which had been progressing for the last week or so, then it might as well be for some good and useful purpose. I might be, in a sense, the agent of Providence! If it were otherwise; if it were the evil work of some discarnate spirit, or something of the sort, well, every Sunday since my childhood, in church, I had recited the Creed, and so admitted, along with the clergy and the rest of the congregation, that God our Father had created all things,—visible and invisible! If it were this part of His creation at work, for any purpose, then He was stronger than they. I said a brief prayer before turning off that light, and put my trust in Him. It may appear to some a bit old-fashioned,—even Victorian! But He does not change along with the current fashions of human thought about Him, and this "human thought," and "the modern mind," and all the rest of it, does not mean the vast, the overwhelming majority of people. It involves only a few dozen prideful "intellectuals" at best, or worst!

I switched off the light, and, already clearer, I saw what must have been Old Morris, getting into bed.

I had interviewed old Mr. Bonesteel, the chief government surveyor, a gentleman of parts and much experience, a West Indian born on this island. Mr. Bonesteel, in response to my guarded enquiries,—for I had, of course, already suspected Old Morris; was not my house still called his?—had stated that he remembered Old Morris well, in his own remote youth. His description of that personage and this apparition tallied. This, undoubtedly, was Old Morris. That it was someone, was apparent. I felt, somehow, rather relieved to realize that it was he. I knew something about him, you see. Mr. Bonesteel had given me a good description and many anecdotes, quite freely, and as though he enjoyed being called on for information about one of the old-timers like Morris. He had been more reticent, guarded, in fact, when I pressed him for details of Morris' end. That there had been some obscurity,—intentional or otherwise, I could never ascertain,—about the old man, I had already known. Such casual enquiries as I had made on other occasions through natural interest in the person whose name still clung to my house sixty years or more since he had lived in it, had never got me anywhere. I had only gathered what Mr. Bonesteel's more ample account corroborated: that Morris had been eccentric, in some ways, amusingly so. That he had been extraordinarily well-to-do. That he gave occasional large parties, which, contrary to the custom of the hospitable island of St. Croix, were always required to come to a conclusion well before midnight. Why, there was a story of Old Morris almost literally getting rid of a few reluctant guests by one device or another from these parties, a circumstance on which hinged several of the amusing anecdotes of that eccentric person!

Old Morris, as I knew, had not always lived on St. Croix. His youth had been spent in Martinique, in the then smaller and less important town of Fort-de-France. That, of course, was many years before the terrific calamity of the destruction of St. Pierre had taken place, by the eruption of Mt. Pelée. Old Morris, coming to St. Croix in young middle age—forty-five or thereabouts,—had already been accounted a rich man. He had been engaged in no business. He was a planter, not a store-keeper, had no profession. Where he produced his affluence was one of the local mysteries. His age, it seemed, was the other.

"I suppose," Mr. Bonesteel had said, that Morris was nearer a hundred than ninety, when he,—ah,—died. I was a child of about eight at that time. I shall be seventy next August-month. That, you see, would be about sixty years ago, about 1861, or about the time your Civil War was beginning. Now my father has told me,—he died when I was nineteen,—that Old Morris looked exactly the same when he was a boy! Extraordinary. The Black People used to say—" Mr. Bonesteel fell silent, and his eyes had an old man's dim, far-away look.

"The Black People have some very strange beliefs, Mr. Bonesteel," said I, attempting to prompt him. "A good many of them I have heard about myself, and they interest me very much. What particular—"

Mr. Bonesteel turned his mild, blue eyes upon me, reflectively.

"You must drop in at my house one of these days, Mr. Stewart," said he, mildly. "I have some rare old rum that I'd be glad to have you sample, sir! There's not much of it on the island these days, since Uncle Sam turned his prohibition laws loose on us in 1922."

"Thank you very much indeed, Mr Bonesteel," I replied. "I shall take the first occasion to do so, sir; not that I care especially for 'old rum' except a spoonful in a cup of tea, or in pudding sauce, perhaps; but the pleasure of your company, sir, is always an inducement."

Mr. Bonesteel bowed to me gravely, and I returned his bow from where I satin his airy office in Government House.

"Would you object to mentioning what that 'belief' was, sir?"

A slightly pained expression replaced my old friend's look of hospitality.

"All that is a lot of foolishness!" said he, with something like asperity. He looked at me, contemplatively.

"Not that I believe in such things, you must understand. Still, a man sees a good many things in these islands, in a lifetime, you know! Well, the Black People—" Mr. Bonesteel looked apprehensively about him, as though reluctant to have one of his clerks overhear what he was about to say, and leaned toward me from his chair, lowering his voice to a whisper.

"They said,—it was a remark here and a kind of hint there, you must understand; nothing definite,—that Morris had interfered, down there in Martinique, with some of their queer doings—offended the Zombi,—something of the kind; that Morris had made some kind of conditions—oh, it was very vague, and probably all mixed up!—you know, whereby he was to have a long life and all the money he wanted,—something like that,—and afterward . . .

"Well, Mr. Stewart, you just ask somebody, sometime about Morris' death."

Not another word about Old Morris could I extract out of Mr. Bonesteel.

But of course he had me aroused. I tried Despard, who lives on the other end of the island, a man educated at the Sorbonne, and who knows, it is said, everything there is know about the island and its affairs.

It was much the same with Mr. Despard, who is an entirely different kind of person; younger, for one thing, my old friend the government surveyor.

Mr. Despard smiled, a kind of wry smile. "Old Morris!" said he, reflectively, and paused.

"Might I venture to ask—no offense, my dear sir!—why you wish to rake up such an old matter as Old Morris' death?"

I was a bit nonplused, I confess. Mr. Despard had been perfectly courteous, as he always is, but, somehow, I had not expected such an intervention on his part.

"Why," said I, "I should find it hard to tell you, precisely, Mr. Despard. It is not that I am averse to being frank in the face of such an inquiry as yours, sir. I was not aware that there was anything important,—serious, as your tone implies,—about that matter. Put it down to mere curiosity if you will, and answer or not, as you wish, sir."

I was, perhaps, a little nettled at this unexpected, and, as it then seemed to me, finicky obstruction being placed in my way. What could there be in such a case for this formal reticence,—these verbal safeguards? If it were a "jumbee" story, there was no importance to it. If otherwise, well, I might be regarded by Despard as a person of reasonable discretion. Perhaps Despard was some relative of Old Morris, and there was something a bit off-color about his death. That, too, might account for Mr. Bonesteel's reticence.

"By the way," I enquired, noting Despard's reticence, "might I ask another question, Mr. Despard?"

"Certainly, Mr. Stewart."

"I do not wish to impress you as idly or unduly curious, but—are you and Mr. Bonesteel related in any way?"

"No, sir. We are not related in any way at all, sir."

"Thank you, Mr. Despard," said I, and, bowing to each other after the fashion set here by the Danes, we parted.

I had not learned a thing about Old Morris' death. I went in to see Mrs. Heidenklang. Here, if anywhere, I should find out what was intriguing me.

Mrs. Heidenklang is an ancient Creole lady, relict of a prosperous storekeeper, who lives, surrounded by a certain state of her own, propped up in bed in an environment of a stupendous quantity of lacy things and gauzy ruffles. I did not intend to mention Old Morris to her, but only to get some information about the Zombi, if that should be possible.

I found the old lady, surrounded by her ruffles and lace things, in one of her good days. Her health has been precarious for twenty years!

It was not difficult to get her talking about the Zombi.

"Yes," said Mrs. Heidenklang, "it is extraordinary how the old beliefs and the old words cling in their minds! Why, Mr. Stewart, I was hearing about a trial in the police court a few days ago. One old Black woman had summoned another for abusive language. On the witness stand the complaining old woman said: 'She cahl me a wuthless ole Cartagene, sir!' Now, think of that! Carthage was destroyed 'way back in the days of Cato the Elder, you know, Mr. Stewart! The greatest town of all Africa. To be a Carthaginian meant to be a sea-robber,—a pirate: that is, a thief. One old woman on this island, more than two thousand years afterward, wishes to call another a thief, and the word 'Cartagene' is the word she naturally uses! I suppose that has persisted on the West Coast and throughout all those village dialects in Africa without a break, all these centuries! The Zombi of the French islands? Yes, Mr. Stewart. There are some extraordinary beliefs. Why, perhaps you've heard mention made of Old Morris, Mr. Stewart. He used to live in your house, you know?"

I held my breath. Here was a possible trove. I nodded my head. I did not dare to speak!

"Well, Old Morris, you see, lived most of his earlier days in Martinique, and, it is said, he had a somewhat adventurous life there, Mr. Stewart. Just what he did or how he got himself involved, seems never to have been made clear, but—in some way, Mr. Stewart, the Black People believe Morris got himself involved with a very powerful 'Jumbee,' and that is where what I said about the persistence of ancient beliefs comes in. Look on that table there, among those photographs, Mr. Stewart. There! that's the place. I wish I were able to get up and assist you. These maids! Everything askew, I have no doubt! Do you observe a kind of fish-headed thing, about as big as the palm of your hand? Yes! that is it!"

I found the "fish-headed thing" and carried it over to Mrs. Heidenklang, She took it in her hand and looked at it. It lacked a nose, but otherwise it was intact, a strange, uncouth-looking little godling, made of anciently-polished volcanic stone, with huge, protruding eyes, small, humanlike ears, and what must have been a nose like a Tortola jack-fish, or a black witch-bird, with its parrot beak.

"Now that," continued Mrs. Heidenklang, "is one of the very ancient household gods of the aborigines of Martinique, and you will observe the likeness in the idea to the *Lares* and *Penates* of your school-Latin days. Whether this is a *lar* or a *penate,* I can not tell," and the old lady paused to smile at her little joke, "but at any rate he is a representation of something very powerful,—a fish-god of the Caribs. There's something Egyptian about the idea, too, I've always suspected; and, Mr. Stewart, a Carib or an Arawak Indian,—there were both in these islands, you know,—looked much like an ancient Egyptian; perhaps half like your Zuñi or Aztec Indians, and half Egyptian, would be a fair statement of his appearance. These fish-gods had men's bodies, you see, precisely like the hawk-headed and jackal-headed deities of ancient Egypt.

"It was one of those, the Black People say, with which Mr. Morris got himself mixed up,—'Gahd knows' as they say-how! And, Mr. Stewart, they say, his death was terrible! The particulars I've never heard, but my father knew, and he was sick for several days, after seeing Mr. Morris' body. Extraordlnary, Isn't it? And when are you coming this way again, Mr. Stewart? Do drop in and call on an old lady."

I felt that I was progressing.

The next time I saw Mr. Bonesteel, which was that very evening, I stopped him on the street and asked for a word with him.

"What was the date, or the approximate date, Mr. Bonesteel, of Mr. Morris' death? Could you recall that, sir?"

Mr. Bonesteel paused and considered.

"It was just before Christmas," said he. "I remember it not so much by Christmas as by the races, which always take place the day after Christmas. Morris had entered his sorrel mare Santurce, and, as he left no heirs, there was no one who 'owned' Santurce, and she had to be withdrawn from the races. It affected the betting very materially and a good many persons were annoyed about it, but there wasn't anything that could be done."

I thanked Mr. Bonesteel, and not without reason, for his answer had fitted into something that had been growing in my mind. Christmas was only eight days off. This drama of the furniture and Old Morris getting into bed, I thought (and not unnaturally, it seems to me), might be a kind of re-enactment of the tragedy of his death. If I had the courage to watch, night after night, I might be relieved of the necessity of asking any questions. I might witness whatever had occurred, in some weird reproduction, engineered, God knows how!

For three nights now, I had seen the phenomenon of Morris getting into bed repeated, and each time it was clearer. I had sketched him into my drawing, a short, squat figure, rather stooped and fat, but possessed of a strange, gorillalike energy. His movements, as he walked toward the bed, seized the edge of the mosquito-netting and climbed in, were, somehow, full of *power,* which was the more apparent since these were ordinary motions. One could not help imagining that Old Morris would have been a tough customer to tackle, for all his alleged age!

This evening, at the hour when this phenomenon was accustomed to enact itself, that is, about eleven o'clock, I watched again. The scene was very much clearer, and I observed something I had not noticed before. Old Morris' simulacrum paused just before seizing the edge of the netting, raised its eyes, and began, with its right hand, a motion precisely like one who is about to sign himself with the cross. The motion was abruptly arrested, however, only the first of the four touches on the body being made.

I saw, too, something of the expression of the face that night, for the first time. At the moment of making the arrested sign, it was one of despairing horror. Immediately afterward, as this motion appeared to be abandoned for the abrupt clutching of the lower edge of the mosquito-net, it changed into a look of ferocious stubbornness, of almost savage self-confidence. I lost the facial expression as the appearance sank down upon the bed and pulled the ghostly bedclothes over itself.

Three nights later, when all this had become as greatly intensified as had the clearing-up process that had affected the furniture, I observed another motion, or what might be taken for the faint foreshadowing of another motion. This was not on the part of Old Morris. It made itself apparent as lightly and elusively as the swift flight of a moth across the reflection of a lamp, over near the bedroom door (the doors in my house are more than ten feet high, in fourteen-foot-high walls), a mere flicker of something,—something entering the room. I looked, and peered at that corner, straining my eyes, but nothing could I see save what I might describe as an intensification of the black shadow in that corner near the door, vaguely formed like a slim human figure, though grossly out of all human proportion. The vague shadow looked purple against the black. It was about ten feet high, and otherwise as though cast by an incredibly tall, thin human being.

I made nothing of it then; and again, despite all this cumulative experience with the strange shadows of my bedroom, attributed this last phenomenon to my eyes. It was too vague to be at that time accounted otherwise than as a mere subjective effect.

But the night following, I watched for it at the proper moment in the sequence of Old Morris' movements as he got into bed, and this time it was distinctly clearer. The shadow, it was, of some monstrous shape, ten feet tall, long, angular, of vaguely human appearance, though even in its merely shadowed form, somehow cruelly, strangely inhuman! I can not describe the cold horror of its realization. The head-part was, relatively to the proportions of the body, short and broad, like a pumpkin head of a "man" made of sticks by boys, to frighten passers-by on Hallowe'en.

The next evening I was out again to an entertainment at the residence of one of my hospitable friends, and arrived home after midnight. There stood the ghostly furniture, there on the bed was the form of the apparently sleeping Old Morris, and there in the corner stood the shadow, little changed from last night's appearance.

The next night would be pretty close to the date of Old Morris' death. It would be that night, or the next at latest according to Mr. Bonesteel's statement. The next day I could not avoid the sensation of something impending!

I entered my room and turned off the light a little before eleven, seated myself, and waited.

The furniture tonight was, to my vision, absolutely indistinguishable from reality. This statement may sound somewhat strange, for it will be remembered that I was sitting in the dark. Approximating terms again, I may say, however, that the furniture was visible in a light of its own, a kind of "phosphorescence," which apparently emanated from it. Certainly there was no natural source of light. Perhaps I may express the matter thus: that light and darkness were reversed in the case of this ghostly bed, bureau, wardrobe, and chairs. When actual light was turned on, they disappeared. In darkness, which, of course, is the absence of physical light, they emerged. That is the nearest I can get to it. At any rate, tonight the furniture was entirely, perfectly, visible to me.

Old Morris came in at the usual time. I could see him with a clarity exactly comparable to what I have said about the furniture. He made his slight pause, his arrested motion of the right hand, and then, as usual, cast from him, according to his expression, the desire for that protective gesture, and reached a hard-looking, gnarled fist out to take hold of the mosquito-netting.

As he did so, a fearful thing leaped upon him, a thing out of the corner by the high doorway,—the dreadful, purplish shadow-thing. I had not been looking in that direction, and while I had not forgotten this newest of the strange items in this fantasmagoria which had been repeating itself before my eyes for many nights, I was wholly unprepared for its sudden appearance and malignant activity.

I have said the shadow was purplish against black. Now that it had taken form, as the furniture and Old Morris himself had taken form, I observed that this purplish coloration was actual. It was a glistening, humanlike, almost metallic-appearing thing, certainly ten feet high, completely covered with great, iridescent fish-scales, each perhaps four square inches in area, which shimmered as it leaped across the room.

I saw it for only a matter of a second or two. I saw It clutch surely and with a deadly malignity, the hunched body of Old Morris, from behind, just, you will remember, as the old man was about to climb into his bed. The dreadful thing turned him about as a wasp turns a fly, in great, flail-like, glistening arms, and never, to the day of my death, do I ever expect to be free of the look on Old Morris' face,—a look of a lost soul who knows that there is no hope for him in this world or the next,—as the great, squat, rounded head, a head precisely like that of Mrs. Heidenklang's little fish-jumbee, descended, revealing to my horrified sight one glimpse of a huge, scythe like parrot-beak which it used, with a nodding motion of the ugly head, to plunge into its writhing victim's breast, with a tearing motion like the barracuda when it attacks and tears.

I fainted then, for that was the last of the fearful picture which I can remember.

I awakened a little after one o'clock, in a dark and empty room peopled by no ghosts, and with my own, more commonplace, mahogany furniture thinly outlined in the faint light of the new moon which was shining cleanly in a starry sky. The fresh night-wind stirred the netting of my bed. I rose, shakily, and went and leaned out of the window, and lit and puffed rapidly at a cigarette, which perhaps did something to settle my jangling nerves.

The next morning, with a feeling of loathing which has gradually worn itself out in the course of the months which have now elapsed since my dreadful experience, I took my drawing again, and added as well as I could the fearful scene I had witnessed. The completed picture was a horror, crude as is my work in this direction. I wanted to destroy it, but I did not, and I laid it away under some unused clothing in one of the large drawers of my bedroom wardrobe.

Three days later, just after Christmas, I observed Despard's car driving through the streets, the driver being alone. I stopped the boy and asked him where Mr. Despard was at the moment. The driver told me Mr. Despard was having breakfast,—the West Indian midday meal,—with Mr. Bonesteel at that gentleman's house on the Prince's Cross Street. I thanked him and went home. I took out the drawing, folded it, and placed it in the inside breast pocket of my coat, and started for Bonesteel's house.

I arrived fifteen minutes or so before the breakfast hour, and was pleasantly received by my old friend and his guest. Mr. Bonesteel pressed me to join them at breakfast, but I declined

Mr. Bonesteel brought in a swizzel, compounded of his very old rum, and after partaking of this in ceremonious fashion, I engaged the attention of both gentlemen.

"Gentlemen," said I, "I trust that you will not regard me as too much of a bore, but I have, I believe, a legitimate reason for asking you if you will tell me the manner in which the gentleman known as Old Morris, who once occupied my house, met his death."

I stopped there, and immediately discovered that I had thrown my kind old host into a state of embarrassed confusion. Glancing at Mr. Despard, I saw at once that if I had not actually offended him, I had, by my question, at least put him "on his dignity." He was looking at me severely, rather, and I confess that for a moment I felt a bit like a schoolboy. Mr. Bonesteel caught something of this atmosphere, and looked helplessly at Despard. Both men shifted uneasily in their chairs; each waited for the other to speak. Despard, at last, cleared his throat.

"You will excuse me, Mr. Stewart," said he, slowly, "but you have asked a question which for certain reasons, no one, aware of the circumstances, would desire to answer. The reasons are, briefly, that Mr. Morris, in certain respects, was—what shall I say, not to do the matter an injustice?—well, perhaps I might say he was abnormal. I do not mean that he was crazy. He was, though, eccentric. His end was such that stating it would open up a considerable argument, one which agitated this island for a long time after he was found dead. By a kind of general consent, that matter is taboo on the island. That will explain to you why no one wishes to answer your question. I am free to say that Mr. Bonesteel here, in considerable distress, told me that you had asked it of him. You also asked me about it not long ago. I can add only that the manner of Mr. Morris' end was such that—" Mr. Despard hesitated, and looked down, a frown on his brow, at his shoe, which he tapped nervously on the tiled floor of the gallery where we were seated.

"Old Morris, Mr. Stewart," he resumed, after a moment's reflection, in which, I imagined, he was carefully choosing his words, "was, to put it plainly, murdered! There was much discussion over the identity of the murderer, but the most of it, the unpleasant part of the discussion, was rather whether he was killed by human agency or not! Perhaps you will see now, sir, the difficulty of the matter. To say that he was murdered by an ordinary murderer is, to my mind, an impossibility. To assert that some other agency, something abhuman, killed him, opens up the question of one's belief, one's credulity. 'Magic' and occult agencies are, as you are aware, strongly intrenched in the minds of the ignorant people of these islands. None of us cares to admit a similar belief. Does that satisfy you, Mr. Stewart, and will you let the matter rest there, sir?"

I drew out the picture, and, without unfolding it, laid it across my knees. I nodded to Mr. Despard, and, to our host, asked:

"As a child, Mr. Bonesteel, were you familiar with the arrangement of Mr Morris' bedroom?"

"Yes, sir," replied Mr. Bonesteel, and added: "Ewrybody was! Persons who had never been in the old man's house, crowded in when—" I intercepted a kind of warning look passing from Despard to the speaker. Mr. Bonesteel, looking much embarrassed, looked at me in that helpless fashion I have already mentioned, and remarked that it was hot weather these days!

"Then," said I, "perhaps you will recognize its arrangement and even some of the details of its furnishing," and I unfolded the picture and handed it to Mr. Bonesteel.

If I had anticipated its effect upon the old man, I would have been more discreet, but I confess I was nettled by their attitude. By handing it to Mr. Bonesteel (I could not give it to both of them at once) I did the natural thing, for he was our host. The old man looked at what I had handed him, and (this is the only way I can describe what happened) became, suddenly, as though petrified. His eyes bulged out of his head, his lower jaw dropped and hung open. The paper slipped from his nerveless grasp and fluttered and zigzagged to the floor, landing at Despard's feet. Despard stooped and picked it up, ostensibly to restore it to me, but in doing so, he glanced at it, and had *his* reaction. He leaped frantically to his feet, and positively goggled at the picture, then at me. Oh, I was having my little revenge for their reticence, right enough!

"My God!" shouted Despard. "My God, Mr. Stewart, where did you get such a thing?"

Mr. Bonesteel drew in a deep breath, the first, it seemed, for sixty seconds, and added his word.

"Oh my God!" muttered the old man, shakily. "Mr. Stewart, Mr. Stewart! what is it, what is it? where—"

"It is a Martinique fish-zombi, what is known to professional occult investigators like Elliott O'Donnell and William Hope Hodgson as an 'elemental'," I explained, calmly. "It is a representation of how poor Mr. Morris actually met his death; until now, as I understand it, a purely conjectural matter. Christiansted is built on the ruins of French Bassin, you will remember," I added. "It is a very likely spot for an 'elemental'!"

"But, but," almost shouted Mr. Despard, "Mr. Stewart, where did you get this, its—"

"I made it," said I, quietly, folding up the picture and placing it back in my inside pocket.

"But how—?" this from both Despard and Bonesteel, speaking in unison.

"I saw it happen, you see," I replied, taking my hat, bowing formally to both gentlemen, and murmuring my regret at not being able to remain for breakfast, I departed.

And as I reached the bottom of Mr. Bonesteel's gallery steps and turned along the street in the direction Of Old Morris' house, where I live, I could hear their voices speaking together:

"But how, how—?" This was Bonesteel.

"Why, why—?" And that was Despard.

CASSIUS

MY HOUSE-MAN, Stephen Penn, who presided over the staff of my residence in St Thomas, was not, strictly speaking, a native of that city. Penn came from the neighboring island of St Jan. It is one of the ancient West Indian names, although there remain in the islands nowadays no Caucasians to bear that honorable cognomen.

Stephen's travels, however, had not been limited to the crossing from St Jan—which, incidentally, is the authentic scene of R. L Stevenson's *Treasure Island*—which lies little more than a rowboat's journey away from the capital of the Virgin Islands. Stephen had been "down the Islands," which means that he had been actually as far from home as Trinidad, or perhaps, British Guiana, down through the great sweep of former mountaintops, submerged by some vast, cataclysmic, prehistoric inundation and named the Bow of Ulysses by some fanciful, antique geographer. That odyssey of humble Stephen Penn had taken place because of his love for ships. He had had various jobs afloat and his exact knowledge of the house-man's art had been learned under various man-driving ship's stewards.

During this preliminary training for his life's work, Stephen had made many acquaintances. One of these, an upstanding, slim, parchment-colored Negro of thirty or so, was Brutus Hellman. Brutus, like Stephen, had settled down in St. Thomas as a house-man. It was, in fact, Stephen who had talked him into leaving his native British Antigua, to try his luck in our American Virgin Islands. Stephen had secured for him his first job in St. Thomas, in the household of a naval officer.

For this friend of his youthful days, Stephen continued to feel a certain sense of responsibility; because, when Brutus happened to be abruptly thrown out of employment by the sudden illness and removal by the Naval Department of his employer in the middle of the winter season in St. Thomas, Stephen came to me and requested that his friend

Brutus be allowed to come to me "on board-wages" until he was able to secure another place.

I acquiesced. I knew Brutus as a first-rate house-man. I was glad to give him a hand, to oblige the always agreeable and highly efficient Stephen, and, indeed, to have so skilful a servant added to my little staff in my bachelor quarters. I arranged for something more substantial than the remuneration asked for, and Brutus Hellman added his skilled services to those of the admirable Stephen. I was very well served that season and never had any occasion to regret what both men alluded to as my "very great kindness!"

It was not long after Brutus Hellman had moved his simple belongings into one of the servants'-quarters cabins in my stone-paved yard, that I had another opportunity to do something for him. It was Stephen once more who presented his friend's case to me. Brutus, it appeared, had need of a minor operation, and, Negro-like, the two of them, talking the matter over between themselves, had decided to ask me, their present patron, to arrange it.

I did so, with my friend, Dr. Pelletier, Chief Surgeon, in charge of our Naval Station Hospital and regarded in Naval circles as the best man in the Medical Corps. I had not inquired about the nature of Brutus' affliction. Stephen had stressed the minor aspect of the required surgery, and that was all I mentioned to Dr. Pelletier.

It is quite possible that if Dr. Pelletier had not been going to Porto Rico on Thursday of that week, this narrative, the record of one of the most curious experiences I have ever had, would never have been set down. If Pelletier, his mind set on sailing at eleven, had not merely walked out of his operating-room as soon as he had finished with Brutus a little after eight that Thursday morning, left the dressing of the slight wound upon Brutus' groin to be performed by his assistants, then that incredible affair which I can only describe as the persecution of the unfortunate Brutus Hellman would never have taken place.

It was on Wednesday, about two P. M., that I telephoned to Dr. Pelletier to ask him to perform an operation on Brutus.

"Send him over to the hospital this afternoon," Pelletier had answered, "And I'll look him over about five and operate the first thing in the morning—if there is any need for an operation! I'm leaving for San Juan at eleven, for a week."

I thanked him and went upstairs to my siesta, after giving Stephen the message to Brutus, who started off for the hospital about an hour later. He remained in the hospital until the following Sunday afternoon. He was entirely recovered from the operation, he reported. It had been a very slight affair, really, merely the removal of some kind of growth. He thanked me for my part in it when he came to announce dinner while I was reading on the gallery.

It was on the Saturday morning, the day before Brutus got back, that I discovered something very curious in an obscure corner of my house-yard, just around the corner of the wall of the three small cabins which occupy its north side. These cabins were tenantless except for the one at the east end of the row. That one was Brutus Hellman's. Stephen Penn, like my cook, washer, and scullery-maid, lived somewhere in the town.

I had been looking over the yard which was paved with old-fashioned flagging. I found it an excellent condition, weeded, freshly swept, and clean. The three stone servants'-cubicles had been recently white-washed and glistened like cake-icing in the morning sun. I looked over this portion of my domain with approval, for I like things shipshape. I glanced into the two narrow air spaces between the little, two-room houses. There were no cobwebs visible. Then I took a look around the east corner of Brutus Hellman's little house where there was a narrow passageway between the house and the high wall of antique Dutch brick, and there, well in towards the north wall, I saw on the ground what I first took to be a discarded toy which some child had thrown there, probably, it occurred to me, over the wall at the back of the stone cabins.

It looked like a doll's house, which, if it had been thrown there, had happened to land right-side-up. It looked more or less like one of the quaint old-fashioned beehives one still sees occasionally in the conservative Lesser Antilles. But it could hardly be a beehive. It was far too small.

My curiosity mildly aroused, I stepped into the alleyway and looked down at the odd little thing. Seen from where I stopped it rewarded scrutiny. For it was, although made in a somewhat bungling way, a reproduction of an African village hut, thatched, circular, conical. The thatching, I suspected, had formerly been most of the business-end of a small house-broom of tine twigs tied together around the end of a stick. The little house's upright "logs" were a heterogenous medley of little round sticks among which I recognized three dilapidated lead pencils and the broken-off handle of a tooth-brush. These details will serve to indicate its size and to justify my original conclusion that the thing was a rather cleverly made child's toy. How such a thing had got into my yard unless over the wall, was an unimportant little mystery. The little hut, from the ground up to its thatched peak, stood about seven inches in height. Its diameter was, perhaps, eight or nine inches.

My first reaction was to pick it up, look at it more closely, and then throw it into the wire cage in another corner of the yard where Stephen burned up waste paper and scraps at frequent intervals. The thing was plainly a discarded toy, and had no business cluttering up my spotless yard. Then I suddenly remembered the washer's pick'ny, a small, silent, very black child of six or seven, who sometimes played quietly in the yard while his stout mother toiled over the washtub set up on a backless chair near the kitchen door where she could keep up a continuous stream of chatter with my cook.

I stayed my hand accordingly. Quite likely this little thatched hut was a valued item of that pick'ny's possessions. Thinking pleasantly to surprise little Aesculapius, or whatever the child's name might be, I took from my pocket a fifty-bit piece—value ten cents—intending to place the coin inside the little house, through its rounded, low entranceway.

Stooping down, I shoved the coin through the doorway, and, as I did so, something suddenly scuttered about inside the hut, and pinched viciously at the ends of my thumb and forefinger.

I was, naturally, startled. I snatched my fingers away, and stood hastily erect. A mouse, perhaps even a rat, inside there! I glanced at my fingers. There was no marks on them. The skin was not broken. The rodent's vicious little sharp teeth had fortunately missed their grip as he snapped at me, intruding on his sacred privacy. Wondering a little I stepped out of the alleyway and into the sunny, open yard, somewhat

upset at this Lilliputian   *contretemps,*   and resolved upon telling Stephen to see to it that there was no ugly rodent there when next little Aesculapius should retrieve his plaything.

But when I arrived at the gallery steps my friend Colonel Lorriquer's car was just drawing up before the house, and, in hastening to greet welcome early-morning callers and later in accepting Mrs. Lorriquer's invitation to dinner and contract at their house that evening, the little hut and its unpleasant inhabitant were driven wholly out of my mind.

I did not think of it again until several days later, on the night when my premises had become the theater for one of the most inexplicable, terrifying and uncanny happenings I have ever experienced.

My gallery is a very pleasant place to sit evenings, except in that spring period during which the West Indian candle-moths hatch in their myriads and, for several successive days, make it impossible to sit outdoors in any lighted, unscreened place.

It was much too early for the candle-moths, however, at the time I am speaking of, and on the evening of that Sunday upon which Brutus Hellman returned from the hospital, a party of four persons including myself, occupied the gallery.

The other man was Arthur Carswell, over from Hayti on a short visit. The two ladies were Mrs. Spencer, Colonel Lorriquer's widowed daughter, and her friend, Mrs. Squire. We had dined an hour previously at the Grand Hotel as guests of Carswell, and, having taken our coffee at my house, were remaining outdoors on the gallery "for a breath of air" on a rather warm and sultry February evening. We were sitting, quietly talking in a rather desultory manner, all of us unspokenly reluctant to move inside the house for a projected evening at contract.

It was, as I recall the hour, about nine o'clock, the night warm, as I have said, and very still. Above, in a cloudless sky of luminous indigo, the tropical stars glowed enormous. The intoxicating sweet odors of white jessamine and tuberoses made the still air redolent. No sound, except an occasional rather languid remark from one of ourselves, broke the exquisite, balmy stillness.

Then, all at once, without any warning and with an abruptness which caused Carswell and me to stand up, the exquisite perfection of the night was rudely shattered by an appalling, sustained scream of sheer mortal terror.

That scream inaugurated what seems to me as I look back upon the next few days, to be one of the most unnerving, devastating, and generally horrible periods I can recall in a lifetime not devoid of adventure. I formulated at that time, and still retain, mentally, a phrase descriptive of it. It was "the Reign of Terror."

Carswell and I, following the direction of the scream, rushed down the outer gallery steps and back through the yard towards the negro-cabins. As I have mentioned, only one of these was occupied, Brutus Hellman's. As we rounded the corner of the house a faint light—it was Brutus' oil lamp—appeared in the form of a wide vertical strip at the entrance of the occupied cabin. To that we ran as to a beacon, and pushed into the room.

The lamp, newly lighted, and smoking, its glass chimney set on askew as though in great haste, dimly illuminated a strange scene. Doubled up and sitting on the side of his bed, the bedclothes near the bed's foot lumped together where he had flung them, cowered Brutus. His face was a dull, ashen gray in the smokey light, his back was bent, his hands clasped tightly about his shin. And, from between those clenched hands, a steady stream of blood stained the white sheet which hung over the bed's edge and spread below into a small pool on the cabin room's stone-paved floor.

Brutus, groaning dismally, rocked back and forth, clutching his leg. The lamp smoked steadily, defiling the close air, while, incongruously, through the now open doorway poured streams and great pulsing breaths of night-blooming tropical flowers, mingling strangely with the hot, acrid odor of the smoking lampwick.

Carswell went directly to the lamp, straightened the chimney, turned down the flame. The lamp ceased its ugly reek and the air of the cabin cleared as Carswell, turning away from the lamp, threw wide the shutters of the large window which, like most West Indian Negroes, Brutus had closed against the "night air" when he retired.

I gave my attention directly to the man, and by the time the air had cleared somewhat I had him over on his back in a reclining position, and with a great strip torn from one of his bedsheets, was binding up the ugly deep little wound in the lower muscle of his leg just at the outside of the shinbone. I pulled the improvised bandage tight, and the flow of blood ceased, and Brutus, his mind probably somewhat relieved by this timely aid, put an end to his moaning, and turned his ashy face up to mine.

"Did you see it, sar?" he inquired, biting back the trembling of his mouth.

I paid practically no attention to this remark. Indeed, I barely heard it. I was, you see, very busily engaged in staunching the flow of blood. Brutus had already lost a considerable quantity, and my rough bandaging was directed entirely to the end of stopping this. Instead of replying to Brutus' question I turned to Carswell, who had finished with the lamp and the window, and now stood by, ready to lend a hand in his efficient way.

"Run up to the bathroom, will you, Carswell, and bring me a couple of rolls of bandage, from the medicine closet, and a bottle of mercurochrome." Carswell disappeared on this errand and I sat, holding my hands tightly around Brutus' leg, just above the bandage. Then he repeated his question, and this time I paid attention to what he was saying.

"See what, Brutus?" I inquired, and looked at him, almost for the first time—into his eyes, I mean. Hitherto I had been looking at my bandaging.

I saw a stark terror in those eyes.

"It," said Brutus; "de T'ing, sar."

I sat on the side of the bed and looked at him. I was, naturally, puzzled.

"What thing, Brutus?" I asked, very quietly, almost soothingly. Such terror possessed my second house-man that, I considered, he must, for the time being, be treated like a frightened child.

"De T'ing what attack me, sar," explained Brutus.

"What was it like?" I countered. "Do you mean it is still here—in your room?"

At that Brutus very nearly collapsed. His eyes rolled up and their irises nearly disappeared; he shuddered as though with a violent chill, from head to foot. I let go his leg. The blood would be no longer flowing,

I felt sure, under that tight bandaging of mine. I turned back the bed-clothes, rolled poor Brutus under them, tucked him in. I took his limp hands and rubbed them smartly. At this instant Carswell came in through the still open doorway, his hands full of first-aid material. This he laid without a word on the bed beside me, and stood, looking at Brutus, slightly shaking his head. I turned to him.

"And would you mind bringing some brandy, old man? He's rather down and out, I'm afraid—trembling from head to foot."

"It's the reaction, of course," remarked Carswell quietly. "I have the brandy here." The efficient fellow drew a small flask from his jacket pocket, uncorked it, and poured out a dose in the small silver cup which covered the patent stopper.

I raised Brutus' head from the pillow, his teeth audibly chattering as I did so, and just as I was getting the brandy between his lips, there came a slight scuttering sound from under the bed, and something, a small, dark, sinister-looking animal of about the size of a mongoose, dashed on all fours across the open space between the bed's corner and the still open doorway and disappeared into the night outside. Without a word Carswell ran after it, turning sharply to the left and running past the open window. I dropped the empty brandy cup, lowered Brutus' head hastily to its pillow, and dashed out of the cabin. Carswell was at the end of the cabins, his flashlight stabbing the narrow alleyway where I had found the miniature African hut. I ran up to him.

"It went up here," said Carswell laconically.

I stood beside him in silence, my hand on his shoulder. He brightened every nook and cranny of the narrow alleyway with his light. There was nothing, nothing alive, to be seen. The Thing had had, of course, ample time to turn some hidden corner behind the cabins, to bury itself out of sight in some accustomed hiding-place, even to climb over the high, rough-surfaced back wall. Carswell brought his flashlight to rest finally on the little hut-like thing which still stood in the alleyway.

"What's that?" he inquired. "Looks like some child's toy."

"That's what I supposed when I discovered it," I answered. "I imag-ine it belongs to the washer's pickaninny." We stepped into the alleyway. It was not quite wide enough for us to walk abreast. Carswell followed me in. I turned over the little hut with my foot. There was nothing under it. I daresay the possibility of this as a cache for the Thing had occurred to Carswell and me simultaneously. The Thing, mongoose, or whatever it was, had got clean away.

We returned to the cabin and found Brutus recovering from his ague-like trembling fit. His eyes were calmer now. The reassurance of our presence, the bandaging, had had effect. Brutus proceeded to thank us for what we had done for him.

Helped by Carswell, I gingerly removed my rough bandage. The blood about that ugly bite—for a bite it certainly was, with unmistakable tooth-marks around its badly torn edges—was clotted now. The flow had ceased. We poured mercurochrome over and through the wound, disinfecting it, and then I placed two entire rolls of three-inch bandage about Brutus' wounded ankle. Then, with various encouragements and reassurances, we left him, the lamp still burning at his request, and went back to the ladies.

Our contract game was, somehow, a jumpy one, the ladies having been considerably upset by the scare down there in the yard, and we concluded it early, Carswell driving Mrs. Spencer home and I walking down the hill with Mrs. Squire to the Grand Hotel where she was spending that winter.

It was still several minutes short of midnight when I returned, after a slow walk up the hill, to my house. I had been thinking of the incident all the way up the hill. I determined to look in upon Brutus Hellman before retiring, but first I went up to my bedroom and loaded a small automatic pistol, and this I carried with me when I went down to the cabins in the yard. Brutus' light was still going, and he was awake, for he responded instantly to my tap on his door.

I went in and talked with the man for a few minutes. I left him the gun, which he placed carefully under his pillow. At the door I turned and addressed him:

"How do you suppose the thing—whatever it was that attacked you, Brutus—could have got in, with everything closed up tight?"

Brutus replied that he had been thinking of this himself and had come to the conclusion that "de T'ing" had concealed itself in the cabin before he had retired and closed the window and door. He expressed himself as uneasy with the window open, as Carswell and I had left it.

"But, man, you should have the fresh air while you sleep. You don't want your place closed up like a field-laborer's, do you?" said I, rallyingly. Brutus grinned.

"No, sar," said he, slowly, "ain't dat I be afeared of de Jumbee! I daresay it born in de blood, sar. I is close up everyt'ing by instinct! Besides, sar, now dat de T'ing attackin' me, p'raps bes' to have the window close up tightly. Den de T'ing cyant possibly mek an entrance 'pon me!"

I assured Brutus that the most agile mongoose could hardly clamber up that smooth, whitewashed wall outside and come in that window. Brutus smiled, but shook his head nevertheless.

"'Tain't a mongoose, nor a rat, neither, sar," he remarked, as he settled himself for rest under the bed-clothes.

"What do you think it is, then?" I inquired.

"Only de good Gawd know, sar," replied Brutus cryptically.

I was perhaps half-way across the house-yard on my way to turn in when my ears were assailed by precisely one of those suppressed combinations of squeals and grunts which John Masefield describes as presaging an animal tragedy under the hedge of an English countryside on a moonlit summer night. Something—a brief, ruthless combat for food or blood, between two small ground animals—was going on somewhere in the vicinity. I paused, listened, my senses the more readily attuned to this bitter duel because of what had happened in Brutus' cabin. As I paused, the squeals of the fighting animals abruptly ceased. One combatant, apparently, had given up the ghost! A grunting noise persisted for a few instants, however, and it made me shudder involuntarily. These sounds were low, essentially bestial, commonplace. Yet there was in them something so savage, albeit on the small scale of our everyday West Indian fauna, as to give me pause. I could feel the beginning of a cold shudder run down my spine under my white drill jacket!

I turned about, almost reluctantly, drawn somehow, in spite of myself, to the scene of combat. The grunts had ceased now, and to my ears, in the quiet of that perfect night of soft airs and moonlight, there came the even more horrible little sound of the tearing of flesh! It was gruesome, quite horrible, well-nigh unbearable. I paused again, a little shaken, it must be confessed, my nerves a trifle unstrung. I was facing in the direction of the ripping sounds now. Then there was silence—complete, tranquil, absolute!

Then I stepped towards the scene of this small conflict, my flashlight sweeping that corner of the yard nearest the small alleyway.

It picked up the victim almost at once, and I thought—I could not be quite sure—that I saw at the very edge of the circle of illumination, the scrambling flight of the victor. The victim was commonplace. It was the body, still slightly palpitating, of a large, well-nourished rat. The dead rat lay well out in the yard, its freshly drawn vital fluid staining a wide smear on the flagstone which supported it—a ghastly-looking affair. I looked down at it curiously. It had indeed, been a ruthless attack to which this lowly creature had succumbed. Its throat was torn out, it was disembowelled, riven terrifically. I stepped back to Brutus' cabin, went in, and picked up from a pile of them on his bureau a copy of one of our small-sheet local newspapers. With this, nodding smilingly at Brutus I proceeded once more to the scene of carnage. I had an idea. I laid the paper down, kicked the body of the rat upon it with my foot, and, picking up the paper, carried the dead rat into Brutus' cabin. I turned up his lamp and carried it over to the bedside.

"Do you suppose this was your animal, Brutus?" I asked. "If so, you seem to be pretty well avenged!"

Brutus grinned and looked closely at the riven animal. Then:

"No, sar," he said, slowly, "'Twas no rat whut attacked me, sar. See de t'roat, please, sar. Him ahl tore out, mos' effectively! No, sar. But—I surmise—from de appearance of dis t'roat, de mouf which maim me on de laig was de same mouf whut completely ruin dis rat!"

And, indeed, judging from the appearance of the rat Brutus' judgment might well be sound.

I wrapped the paper about it, said good night once more to Hellman, carried it out with me, threw it into the metal waste-basket in which the house-trash is burned every morning, and went to bed.

At three minutes past four the next morning I was snatched out of my comfortable bed and a deep sleep by the rattle of successive shots from the wicked little automatic I had left with Brutus. I jumped into my bathrobe, thrust my feet into my slippers, and was downstairs on the run, almost before the remnants of sleep were out of my eyes and brain. I ran out through the kitchen, as the nearest way, and was inside Brutus' cabin before the empty pistol, still clutched in his hand and pointed towards the open window, had ceased smoking. My first words were:

"Did you get It, Brutus?" I was thinking of the thing in terms of "It."

"Yes, sar," returned Brutus, lowering his pistol. "I t'ink I scotch him. sar. Be please to look on de window-sill. P'raps some blood in evidence, sar."

I did so, and found that Brutus' marksmanship was better than I had anticipated when I entrusted him with the gun. To be sure, he had fired off all seven bullets, and, apparently, scored only one hit. A small, single drop of fresh blood lay on the white-painted wooden window-sill. No other trace of the attacker was in evidence. My flashlight revealed no marks, and the smooth, freshly-whitewashed wall outside was unscathed. Unless the Thing had wings—something suddenly touched me on the forehead, something light and delicate. I reached up, grasping. My hand closed around something like a string. I turned the flashlight up and there hung a thin strand of liana stem. I pulled it. It was firmly fastened somewhere up above there. I stepped outside, with one of Brutus' chairs, placed this against the outer wall under the window, and standing on it, raked the eaves with the flashlight. The upper end of the liana stem was looped about a small projection in the gutter, just above the window.

The Thing, apparently, knew enough to resort to this mechanical method for its second attack that night.

Inside, Brutus, somewhat excited over his exploit, found a certain difficulty in describing just what it was that had drawn his aim.

"It hav de appearance of a frog, sar," he vouchsafed. "I is wide awake when de T'ing land himse'f 'pon de sill, an' I have opportunity for takin' an excellent aim, sar." That was the best I could get out of Brutus. I tried to visualize a "Thing" which looked like a frog, being able to master one of our big, ferocious rats and tear out its inner parts and go off with them, not to mention liana stems with loop-knots in them to swing from a roof to an open window, and which could make a wound like the one above Brutus Hellman's ankle. It was rather too much for me. But—the Reign of Terror had begun, and no mistake!

Running over this summary in my mind as I stood and listened to Brutus telling about his marksmanship, it occurred to me, in a somewhat fantastic light, I must admit—the idea of calling in "science" to our aid, forming the fantastic element—that the Thing had left a clue which might well be unmistakable; something which, suitably managed, might easily clear up the mounting mystery.

I went back to the house, broached my medicine closet, and returned to the cabin with a pair of glass microscopic slides. Between these I made a smear of the still fresh and fluid blood on the window-sill, and went back to my room, intending to send the smear later in the morning to Dr. Pelletier's laboratory-man at the Municipal Hospital.

I left the slides there myself, requesting Dr. Brownell to make me an analysis of the specimen with a view to determining its place in the gamut of West Indian fauna, and that afternoon, shortly after the siesta hour, I received a telephone call from the young physician. Dr. Brownell had a certain whimsical cast apparent in his voice which was new to me. He spoke, I thought, rather banteringly.

"Where did you get your specimen, Mr. Canevin?" he inquired. I understood you to say it was the blood of some kind of lower animal."

"Yes," said I, "that was what I understood, Dr. Brownell. Is there something peculiar about it?"

"Well—" said Dr. Brownell slowly, and somewhat banteringly, "yes—and no. The only queer thing about it is that it's—human blood, probably a Negro's."

I managed to thank him, even to say that I did not want the specimen returned, in answer to his query, and we rang off.

The plot, it seemed to me, was, in the language of the tradition of strange occurrences, thickening! This, then, must be Brutus' blood. Brutus' statement, that he had shot at and struck the marauder at his open window, must be imagination—Negro talk! But, even allowing that it was Brutus' blood—there was, certainly, no one else about to supply that drop of fresh fluid which 1 had so carefully scraped up on my two glass slides—how had he got blood, from his wounded lower leg, presumably, on that high window-sill? To what end would the man lie to me on such a subject? Besides, certainly he had shot at something—the pistol was smoking when I got to his room. And then—the liana stem? How was that to be accounted for?

Dr. Brownell's report made the whole thing more complicated than it had been before. Science, which I had so cheerfully invoked, had only served to make this mystery deeper and more inexplicable.

Handicapped by nothing more than a slight limp Brutus Hellman was up and attending to his duties about the house the next day. In response to my careful questioning, he had repeated the story of his shooting in all particulars just as he had recounted that incident to me in the gray hours of the early morning. He had even added a particular which fitted in with the liana stem as the means of ingress. The Thing, he said, had appeared to swing down onto the window-sill from above, as he, awake for the time being between cat-naps, had first seen it and reached for the pistol underneath his pillow and then opened fire.

Nothing happened throughout the day; nor, indeed, during the Reign of Terror as I have called it, did anything untoward occur throughout, except at night. That evening, shortly after eight o'clock, Brutus retired, and Stephen Penn, who had accompanied him to his cabin, reported to me that, in accordance with my suggestion, the two of them had made an exhaustive search for any concealed "Thing" which might have secreted itself about Brutus' premises. They had found nothing, and Brutus, his window open, but provided with a tight-fitting screen which had been installed during the day, had fallen asleep before Stephen left. Penn had carefully closed the cabin door behind him, making sure that it was properly latched.

The attack that night—I had been sleeping "with one eye open"— did not come until two o'clock in the morning. This time Brutus bad no opportunity to use the gun, and so I was not awakened until it was all over. It was, indeed, Brutus calling me softly from the yard at a quarter past two that brought me to my feet and to the window.

"Yes,," said I, "what is it, Brutus?"

"You axed me to inform you, sar, of anything," explained Brutus from the yard.

"Right! What happened? Wait, Brutus, I'll come down," and I hurriedly stepped into bathrobe and slippers.

Brutus was waiting for me at the kitchen door, a hand to his left cheek, holding a handkerchief rolled into a ball. Even in the moonlight I could see that this makeshift dressing was bright red. Brutus, it appeared, had suffered another attack of some kind. I took him into the house and upstairs, and dressed the three wounds in his left cheek in my bathroom. He had been awakened without warning, fifteen minutes before, with a sudden hurt, had straightened up in bed, but not before two more stabs, directly through the cheek, had been delivered. He had only just seen the Thing scrambling down over the foot of the bed, as he came awake under the impetus of these stabs, and, after a hasty search for the attacker had wisely devoted himself to staunching his bleeding face. Then, trembling in every limb, he had stepped out into the yard and come under my window to call me.

The three holes through the man's cheek were of equal size and similar appearance, obviously inflicted by some stabbing implement of about the diameter of a quarter-inch. The first stab, Brutus thought, had been the one highest up, and this one had not only penetrated into the mouth like the others, but had severely scratched the gum of the upper jaw just above his eye-tooth. I talked to him as I dressed these three wounds. "So the Thing must have been concealed inside your room, you think, Brutus?"

"Undoubtedly, sar," returned Brutus. "There was no possible way for it to crawl in 'pon me—de door shut tight, de window-screen undisturb', sar."

The poor fellow was trembling from head to foot with shock and fear, and I accompanied him back to his cabin. He had not lighted his lamp. It was only by the light of the moon that he had seen his assailant disappear over the foot of the bed. He had seized the handkerchief and run out into the yard in his pajamas.

I lit the lamp, determining to have electricity put into the cabin the next day, and, with Brutus' assistance, looked carefully over the room. Nothing, apparently, was hidden anywhere; there was only a little space to search through; Brutus had few belongings; the cabin furniture was adequate but scanty. There were no superfluities, no place, in other words, in which the Thing could hide itself.

Whatever had attacked Brutus was indeed going about its work with vicious cunning and determination.

Brutus turned in, and after sitting beside him for a while, I left the lamp turned down, closed the door, and took my departure.

Brutus did not turn up in the morning, and Stephen Penn, returning from an investigatory visit to the cabin came to me on the gallery about nine o'clock with a face as gray as ashes. He had found Brutus unconscious, the bed soaked in blood, and, along the great pectoral muscle where the right arm joins the body, a long and deep gash from which the unfortunate fellow had, apparently, lost literally quarts of blood. I telephoned for a doctor and hurried to the cabin.

Brutus was conscious upon my arrival, but so weakened from loss of blood as to be quite unable to speak. On the floor, beside the bed, apparently where it had fallen, lay a medium-sized pocket knife, its largest blade open, soaked in blood. Apparently this had been the instrument with which he had been wounded.

The doctor, soon after his arrival; declared a blood-transfusion to be necessary, and this operation was performed at eleven o'clock in the cabin, Stephen contributing a portion of the blood, a young Negro from the town, paid for his service, the rest. After that, and the administration of a nourishing hot drink, Brutus was able to tell us what had happened.

Against his own expectations, he had fallen asleep immediately after my departure, and curiously, had been awakened not by any attack upon him, but by the booming of a *rata* drum from somewhere up in the hills back of the town where some of the Negroes were, doubtless, "making magic," a common enough occurrence in any of the vodu-ridden West India islands. But this, according to Brutus, was no ordinary awakening.

No—for, on the floor, beside his bed, *dancing to the distant drumbeats,* he had seen—It!

That Brutus had possessed some idea of the identity or character of his assailant, I had, previous to this occurrence of his most serious wound, strongly suspected. I had gathered this impression from half a dozen little things, such as his fervid denial that the creature which had bitten him was either a rat or a mongoose; his "Gawd know" when I had asked him what the Thing was like.

Now I understood, clearly of course, that Brutus knew what kind of creature had concealed itself in his room. I even elicited the fact, discovered by him, just how I am quite unaware, that the Thing had hidden under a loose floor board beneath his bed and so escaped detection on the several previous searches.

But to find out from Brutus—the only person who knew—that, indeed, was quite another affair. There can be, I surmise, no human being as consistently and completely shut-mouthed as a West Indian Negro, once such a person has definitely made up his mind to silence on a given subject! And on this subject, Brutus had, it appeared, quite definitely made up his mind. No questions, no cajolery, no urging—even with tears, on the part of his lifelong friend Stephen Penn—could elicit from him the slightest remark bearing on the description or identity of the Thing. I myself used every argument which logic and common-sense presented to my Caucasian mind. I urged his subsequent safety upon Brutus, my earnest desire to protect him, the logical necessity of co-operating, in the stubborn fellow's own obvious interest, with us who had his welfare at heart. Stephen, as I have said, even wept! But all these efforts on our parts, were of no avail. Brutus Hellman resolutely refused to add a single word to what he had already said. He had awakened to the muted booming of the distant drum. He had seen the Thing dancing beside his bed. He had, it appeared, fainted from this shock, whatever the precise nature of that shock may have been, and knew nothing more until he came slowly to a vastly weakened consciousness between Stephen Penn's visit to him late in the morning, and mine which followed it almost at once.

There was one fortunate circumstance. The deep and wide cut which had, apparently, been inflicted upon him with his own pocket-knife—and had been lying, open, by mere chance, on a small tabouret beside his bed—had been delivered lengthwise of the pectoral muscle, not across the muscle. Otherwise the fellow's right arm would have been seriously crippled for life. The major damage he had suffered in this last and most serious attack had been the loss of blood, and this, through my employment of one donor of blood and Stephen Penn's devotion in giving him the remainder, had been virtually repaired.

However, whether he spoke or kept silent, it was plain to me that I had a very definite duty towards Brutus Hellman. I could not, if anything were to be done to prevent it, have him attacked in this way while in my service and living on my premises.

The electricity went in that afternoon, with a pull-switch placed near the hand of whoever slept in the bed, and, later in the day, Stephen Penn brought up on a donkey cart from his town lodging-place, his own bedstead, which he set up in Brutus' room, and his bureau containing the major portion of his belongings, which he placed in the newly-swept and garnished cabin next door. If the Thing repeated its attack that night, it would have Stephen, as well as Brutus, to deal with.

One contribution to our knowledge Stephen made, even before he had actually moved into my yard. This was the instrument with which Brutus had been stabbed through the cheek. He found it cached in the floor-space underneath that loose board where the Thing had hidden itself. He brought it to me, covered with dried blood. It was a rough, small-scale reproduction of an African "assegai," or stabbing-spear. It was made out of an ordinary butcher's hardwood meat-skewer, its head a splinter of pointed glass such as might be picked up anywhere about the town. The head—and this was what caused the resemblance to an "assegai"—was very exactly and neatly bound on to the cleft end of the skewer, with fishline. On the whole, and considered as a piece of work, the "assegai" was a highly creditable job.

It was on the morning of this last-recorded attack on Brutus Hellman during the period between my visit to him and the arrival of the doctor with the man for the blood-transfusion, that I sat down, at my desk, in an attempt to figure out some conclusion from the facts already known. I had progressed somewhat with my theoretical investigation at that time. When later, after Brutus could talk, he mentioned the circumstance of the Thing's dancing there on his cabin floor, to the notes of a drum, in the pouring moonlight which came through his screened window and gave its illumination to the little room, I came to some sort of indeterminate decision. I will recount the steps—they are very brief—which led up to this.

The facts, as I noted them down on paper that day, pointed to a pair of alternatives. Either Brutus Hellman was demented, and had invented his "attacks," having inflicted them upon himself for some inscrutable reason; or—the Thing was possessed of qualities not common among the lower animals! I set the two groups of facts side by side, and compared them.

Carswell and I had actually seen the Thing as It ran out of the cabin that first night. Something, presumably the same Thing, had torn a large rat to pieces. The same Thing had bitten savagely Brutus' lower leg. Brutus' description of it was that it looked "like a frog." Those four facts seemed to indicate one of the lower animals, though its genus and the motive for its attacks were unknown!

On the other hand, there was a divergent set of facts. The Thing had used mechanical means, a liana stem with a looped knot in it, to get into Brutus' cabin through the window. It had used some stabbing instrument, later found, and proving to be a manufactured affair. Again, later, it had used Brutus' knife in its final attack. All these facts pointed to some such animal as a small monkey. This theory was strengthened by the shape of the bites on Brutus' leg and on the rat's throat.

That it was *not* a monkey, however, there was excellent evidence. The Thing looked like a frog. A frog is a very different-looking creature from any known kind of monkey. There were, so far as I knew, no monkeys at the time on the island of St. Thomas.

I added to these sets of facts two other matters: The blood alleged to be drawn from the Thing had, on analysis, turned out to be human blood. The single circumstance pointed very strongly to the insanity theory. On the other hand, Brutus could hardly have placed the fresh blood which I had myself scraped up on my slides, on the windowsill where I found it. Still, he might have done so, if his insanity" were such as to allow for an elaborately "planted" hoax or something of the kind. He could have placed the drop of blood there, drawn from his own body by means of a pin-prick, before he fired the seven cartridges that night. It was possible. But, knowing Brutus, it was so improbable as to be quite absurd.

The final circumstance was the little "African" hut. That, somehow, seemed to fit in with the "assegai." The two naturally went together.

It was a jumble, a puzzle. The more I contrasted and compared these clues, the more impossible the situation became

Well, there was one door open, at least. I decided to go through that door and see where it led me. I sent for Stephen. It was several hours after the blood-transfusion. I had to get some of Brutes' blood for my experiment, but it must be blood drawn previous to the transfusion. Stephen came to see what I wanted.

"Stephen," said I, "I want you to secure from Hellman's soiled things one of those very bloody sheets which you changed on his bed today, and bring it here."

Stephen goggled at me, but went at once on this extraordinary errand. He brought me the sheet. On one of its corners, there was an especially heavy mass of clotted blood. From the underside of this I managed to secure a fresh enough smear on a pair of glass slides, and with these I stepped into my car and ran down to the hospital and asked for Dr. Brownell.

I gave him the slides and asked him to make for me an analysis for the purpose of comparing this blood with the specimen I had given him two days before. My only worry was whether or not they had kept a record of the former analysis, it being a private job and not part of the hospital routine. They had recorded it, however, and Dr. Brownell obligingly made the test for me then and there. Half an hour after he had stepped into the laboratory he came back to me.

"Here are the records," he said. "The two specimens are unquestionably from the same person, presumably a Negro. They are virtually identical."

The blood alleged to be the Thing's, then, was merely Brutus' blood. The strong presumption was, therefore, that Brutus had lost his mind.

Into this necessary conclusion, I attempted to fit the remaining facts. Unfortunately for the sake of any solution, they did not fit! Brutus might, for some insane reason, have inflicted the three sets of wounds upon himself. But Brutus had not made the "African" hut, which had turned up before he was back from the hospital. He had not, presumably, fastened that liana stem outside his window. He had not, certainly, slain that rat, nor could he have "invented" the creature which both Carswell and I had seen, however vaguely, running out of his cabin that night of the first attack.

At the end of all my cogitations, I knew absolutely nothing, except what my own senses had conveyed to me; and these discordant facts I have already set down in their order and sequence, precisely and accurately, as they occurred.

To these I now add the additional fact that upon the night following the last recorded attack on Brutus Hellman nothing whatever happened. Neither he nor Stephen Penn, sleeping side by side in their two beds in the cabin room, was in any way disturbed.

I wished, fervently, that Dr. Pelletier were at hand. I needed someone like him to talk to. Carswell would not answer, somehow. No one would answer. I needed Pelletier, with his incisive mind, his scientific training, his vast knowledge of the West Indies, his open-mindedness to facts wherever these and their contemplation might lead the investigator. I needed Pelletier very badly indeed!

And Pelletier was still over in Porto Rico.

Only one further circumstance, and that, apparently, an irrelevant one, can be added to the facts already narrated—those incongruous facts which did not appear to have any reasonable connection with one another and seemed to be mystifyingly contradictory. The circumstance was related to me by Stephen Penn, and it was nothing more or less than the record of a word, a proper name. This, Stephen alleged, Brutus had repeated, over and over, as, under the effects of the two degrees of temperature which he was carrying as the result of his shock and of the blood-transfusion, he had tossed about restlessly during a portion of the night. That name was, in a sense, a singularly appropriate one for Brutus to utter, even though one would hardly suspect the fellow of having any acquaintance with Roman history, or, indeed, with the works of William Shakespeare!

The name was—Cassius!

I figured that anyone bearing the Christian name, Brutus, must, in the course of a lifetime, have got wind of the original Brutus' side-partner. The two names naturally go together, of course, like Damon and Pythias, David and Jonathan! However, I said nothing about this to Brutus.

I was on the concrete wharf beside the Naval Administration Building long before the *Grebe* arrived from San Juan on the Thursday morning a week after Brutus Hellman's operation.

I wanted to get Pelletier's ear at the earliest possible moment. Nearby, in the waiting line against the wall of the Navy building, Stephen Penn at the wheel, stood my car. I had telephoned Pelletier's man that he need not meet the doctor. I was going to do that myself, to get what facts, whatever explanation Pelletier might have to offer as I drove him through the town and up the precipitous roadways of Denmark Hill to his house at its summit.

My bulky, hard-boiled, genial naval surgeon friend, of the keen, analytical brain and the skillful hands which so often skirted the very edges of death in his operating-room, was unable, however, to accompany me at once upon his arrival. I had to wait more than twenty minutes for him, while others, who had prior claims upon him, interviewed him. At last he broke away from the important ones and heaved his unwieldy bulk into the back seat of my car beside me. Among those who had waylaid him, I recognized Doctors Roots and Maguire, both naval surgeons.

I had not finished my account of the persecution to which Brutus Hellman had been subjected by the time we arrived at the doctor's hilltop abode. I told Stephen to wait for me and finished the story inside the house while Pelletier's houseman was unpacking his traveling valises. Pelletier heard me through in virtual silence, only occasionally interrupting with a pertinent question. When I had finished he lay back in his chair, his eyes closed.

He said nothing for several minutes. Then, his eyes still shut, he raised and slightly waved his big, awkward-looking hand, that hand of such uncanny skill when it held a knife, and began to speak, very slowly and reflectively:

"Dr. Roots mentioned a peculiar circumstance on the wharf."

"Yes?" said I.

"Yes," said Dr. Pelletier. He shifted his ungainly bulk in his big chair, opened his eyes and looked at me. Then, very deliberately:

"Roots reported the disappearance of the thing—it was a parasitic growth—that I removed from your houseman's side a week ago. When they had dressed the fellow and sent him back to the ward Roots intended to look the thing over in the laboratory. It was quite unusual. I'll come to that in a minute. But when he turned to pick it up, it was gone; had quite disappeared. The nurse, Miss Charles, and he looked all over for it, made a very thorough search. That was one of the things he came down for this morning—to report that to me." Once again Pelletier paused, looked at me searchingly, as though studying me carefully. Then he said:

"I understand you to say that the Thing, as you call it, is still at large?"

The incredible possible implication of this statement of the disappearance of the "growth" removed from Hellman's body and the doctor's question, stunned me for an instant. Could he possibly mean to imply—? I stared at him, blankly, for an instant.

"Yes," said I, "it is still at large, and poor Hellman is barricaded in his cabin. As I have told you, I have dressed those bites and gashes myself. He absolutely refuses to go to the hospital again. He lies there, muttering to himself, ash-gray with fear."

"Hm," vouchsafed Dr. Pelletier. "How big would you say the Thing is, Canevin, judging from your glimpse of it and the marks it leaves?"

"About the size, say, of a rat," I answered, "and black. We had that one sight of it, that first night. Carswell and I both saw it scuttering out of Hellman's cabin right under our feet when this horrible business first started."

Dr. Pelletier nodded, slowly. Then he made another remark, apparently irrelevant;

"I had breakfast this morning on board the *Grebe*. Could you give me lunch?" He looked at his watch.

"Of course," I returned. "Are you thinking of—"

"Let's get going," said Dr. Pelletier, heaving himself to his feet.

We started at once, the doctor calling out to his servants that be would not be back for one o'clock "breakfast," and Stephen Penn who had driven us up the hill drove us down again. Arrived at my house we proceeded straight to Hellman's cabin. Dr. Pelletier talked soothingly to the poor fellow while examining those ugly wounds. On several he placed fresh dressings from his professional black bag. When he had finished he drew me outside

"You did well, Canevin," he remarked, reflectively, "in not calling in anybody, dressing those wounds yourself! What people don't know, er—won't hurt 'em!"

He paused after a few steps away from the cabin.

"Show me," he commanded, "which way the Thing ran, that first night."

I indicated the direction, and we walked along the line of it, Pelletier forging ahead, his black bag in his big hand. We reached the corner of the cabin in a few steps, and Pelletier glanced up the alleyway between the cabin's side and the high yard-wall. The little toy house, looking somewhat dilapidated now, still stood where it had been, since I first discovered it. Pelletier did not enter the alleyway. He looked in at the queer little miniature hut.

"Hm," he remarked, his forehead puckered into a thick frowning wrinkle. Then, turning abruptly to me:

"I suppose it must have occurred to you that the Thing lived in that," said he, challengingly.

"Yes—naturally; after it went for my fingers—whatever that creature may have been. Three or four times I've gone in there with a flashlight after one of the attacks on Brutus Hellman; picked it up, even, and looked inside—"

"And the Thing is never there," finished Dr. Pelletier, nodding sagaciously.

"Never," I corroborated.

"Come on up to the gallery," said the doctor, "and I'll tell you what I think."

We proceeded to the gallery at once and Dr. Pelletier, laying down his black bag, caused a lounge-chair to groan and creak beneath his recumbent weight while I went into the house to command the usual West Indian preliminary to a meal.

A few minutes later Dr. Pelletier told me what he thought, according to his promise. His opening remark was in the form of a question; about the very last question anyone in his senses would have regarded as pertinent to the subject in hand.

"Do you know anything about twins, Canevin?" he inquired.

"Twins?" said I. "Twins!" I was greatly puzzled. I had not been expecting any remarks about twins.

"Well," said I, as Dr. Pelletier stared at me gravely, "only what everybody knows about them, I imagine. What about them?"

"There are two types of twins, Canevin—and I don't mean the difference arising out of being separate or attached-at-birth, the 'Siamese' or ordinary types. I mean something far more basic than that accidental division into categories; more fundamental—deeper than that kind of distinction. The two kinds of twins I have reference to are called in biological terminology 'monozygotic' and 'dizygotic,' respectively; those which originate, that is, from one cell, or from two."

"The distinction," I threw in, "which Johannes Lange makes in his study of criminal determinism, his book, *Crime and Destiny.* The one-cell-originated twins, he contends, have identical motives and personalities. If one is a thief, the other has to be! He sets out to prove—and that pompous ass, Haldane, who wrote the foreword, believes it, too—that there is no freewill; that man's moral course is predetermined, inescapable-a kind of scientific Calvinism."

"Precisely, just that," said Dr. Pelletier. "Anyhow, you understand that distinction." I looked at him, still somewhat puzzled.

"Yes," said I, "but still, I don't see its application to this nasty business of Brutus Hellman."

"I was leading up to telling you," said Dr. Pelletier, in his matter-of-fact, forthright fashion of speech; "to telling you, Canevin, that the Thing is undoubtedly, the parasitic, 'Siamese-twin' that I cut away from Brutus Hellman last Thursday morning, and which disappeared out of the operating-room. Also, from the evidence, I'd be inclined to think it is of the 'dizygotic' type. That would not occur, in the case of 'attached' twins, more than once in ten million times!"

He paused at this and looked at me. For my part, after that amazing, that utterly incredible statement, so calmly made, so dispassionately uttered, I could do nothing but sit limply in my chair and gaze woodenly at my guest. I was so astounded that I was incapable of uttering a word. But I did not have to say anything. Dr. Pelletier was speaking again, developing his thesis.

"Put together the known facts, Canevin. It is the scientific method, the only satisfactory method, when you are confronted with a situation like this one. You can do so quite easily, almost at random, here. To begin with, you never found the Thing in that little thatched hut after one of its attacks—did you?"

"No," I managed to murmur, out of a strangely dry mouth. Pelletier's theory held me stultified by its unexpectedness, its utter, weird strangeness. The name, "Cassius," smote my brain. That identical blood—

"If the Thing had been, say, a rat," he continued, "as you supposed when it went for your fingers, it would have gone straight from its attacks on Brutus Hellman to its diggings—the refuge-instinct; holing-up.' But it didn't. You investigated several times and it wasn't inside the little house, although it ran towards it, as you believed, after seeing it start that way the first night; although the creature that went for your hand was there, inside, *before it suspected pursuit.* You see? That gives us a lead, a clue. The Thing possesses a much higher level of intelligence than that of a mere rodent. Do you grasp that significant point, Canevin? The Thing, anticipating pursuit, avoided capture by instinctively outguessing the pursuer. It went towards its diggings but deferred entrance until the pursuer had investigated and gone away. Do you get it?"

I nodded, not desiring to interrupt. I was following Pelletier's thesis eagerly now. He resumed:

"Next—consider those wounds, those bites, on Brutus Hellman. They were never made by any small, ground- dwelling animal, a rodent, like a rat or a mongoose. No; those teeth-marks are those of—well, say, a marmoset or any very small monkey; or, Canevin, *of an unbelievably small human being!"*

Pelletier and I sat and looked at each other. I think that, after an appreciable interval, I was able to nod my head in his direction. Pelletier continued:

"The next point we come to—before going on to something a great deal deeper, Canevin—is the color of the Thing. You saw it. It was only a momentary glimpse, as you say, but you secured enough of an impression to seem pretty positive on that question of its color. Didn't you?"

"Yes," said I, slowly. "It was as black as a derby hat, Pelletier."

"There you have one point definitely settled, then." The doctor was speaking with a judicial note in his voice, the scientist in full stride now. "The well-established ethnic rule, the biological certain in cases of miscegenation between Caucasians or quasi-Caucasians and the Negro or negroid types is that the offspring is never darker than the darker of the two parents. The 'black-baby' tradition, as a 'throw-back' being produced by mulatto or nearly Caucasian parents is a bugaboo,

Canevin, sheer bosh! It doesn't happen that way. It*cannot* happen. It is a biological impossibility, my dear man. Although widely believed, that idea falls into the same category as the ostrich burying its head in the sand and thinking it is concealed! It falls in with the Amazon myth! The 'Amazons' were merely long-haired Scythians, those 'women-warriors' of antiquity. Why, damn it, Canevin, it's like believing in the Centaur to swallow a thing like that."

The doctor had become quite excited over his expression of biological orthodoxy. He glared at me, or appeared to, and lighted a fresh cigarette. Then, considering for a moment, while he inhaled a few preliminary puffs, he resumed:

"You see what that proves, don't you, Canevin?" he inquired, somewhat more calmly now.

"It seems to show," I answered, "since Brutus is very 'clear-colored,' as the Negroes would say, that one of his parents was a black; the other very considerably lighter, perhaps even a pure Caucasian."

"Right, so far," acquiesced the doctor. "And the other inference, in the case of twins—what?"

"That the twins were 'dizygotic,' even though attached," said I, slowly, as the conclusion came clear in my mind after Pelletier's preparatory speech. "Otherwise, of course, if they were the other kind, the mono-cellular or 'monozygotic,' they would have the same coloration, derived from either the dark or the light-skinned parent."

"Precisely," exclaimed Dr. Pelletier. "Now—"

'You mentioned certain other facts," I interrupted, "'more deep-seated,' I think you said. What—"

"I was just coming to those, Canevin. There are, actually, two such considerations which occur to me. First—why did the Thing degenerate, undoubtedly after birth, of course, if there were no pre-natal process of degeneration? They would have been nearly of a size, anyway, when born, I'd suppose. Why did 'It' shrink up into a withered, apparently lifeless little homunculus, while its fellow twin, Brutus Hellman, at-tained to a normal manhood? There are some pretty deep matters in-volved in those queries, Canevin. It was comatose, shrunken, virtually dead while attached"

"Let's see if we can't make a guess at them," I threw in.

"What would *you* say?" countered Dr. Pelletier.

I nodded, and sat silently for several minutes trying to put what was in my mind together in some coherent form so as to express it ad-equately. Then:

"A couple of possibilities occur to me," I began. "One or both of them might account for the divergence. First, the failure of one or more of the ductless glands, very early in the Thing's life after birth. It's the pituitary gland, isn't it, that regulates the physical growth of an infant— that makes him grow normally. If that fails before it has done its full work, about the end of the child's second year, you get a midget. if, on the other hand, it keeps on too long—does not dry up as it should, and cease functioning, its normal task finished—the result is a giant; the child simply goes on growing, bigger and bigger! Am I right, so far? And, I suppose, the cutting process released it from its coma."

"Score one!" said Dr. Pelletier, wagging his head at me. "Go on— what else? There are many cases, of course, of blood-letting ending a coma."

"The second guess is that Brutus had the stronger constitution, and outstripped the other one. It doesn't sound especially scientific, but that sort of thing does happen as I understand it. Beyond those two possible explanations I shouldn't care to risk any more guesses."

"I think both those causes have been operative in this case," said Dr. Pelletier, reflectively. "And, having performed that operation, you see, I think I might add a third, Canevin. It is purely conjectural. I'll admit that frankly, but one outstanding circumstance supports it. I'll come back to that shortly. In short, Canevin, I imagine—my instinct tells me—that almost from the beginning, quite unconsciously, of course, and in the automatic processes of outstripping his twin in physical growth, *Brutus absorbed the other's share* of nutriments.

"I can figure that out, in fact, from several possible angles. The early nursing, for instance! The mother—she was, undoubtedly, the black parent—proud of her 'clear' child, would favor it, nurse it first. There is, besides, always some more or less obscure interplay, some balanced adjustment, between physically attached twins. In this case, God knows how, that invariable 'balance' became disadjusted; the adjustment be-came unbalanced, if you prefer it that way. The mother, too, from whose side the dark twin probably derived its constitution, may very well have been a small, weakly woman. The fair-skinned other parent was probably robust, physically. But, whatever the underlying causes, we know that Brutus grew up to be normal and fully mature, and I know, from that operation, that the Thing I cut away from him was his twin brother, degenerated into an apparently lifeless homunculus, a mere appendage of Brutus, something which, *apparently, had quite lost nearly everything of its basic humanity;* even most of its appearance, Canevin—a Thing to be removed surgically, like a wen."

"It is a terrible idea," said I, slowly, and after an interval. "But, it seems to be the only way to explain, er—the facts! Now tell me, if you please, what is that 'outstanding circumstance' you mentioned which corroborates this, er—theory of yours."

"it is the Thing's motive, Canevin," said Dr Pelletier, very gravely, "allowing, of course, that we are right—that I am right—in assuming for lack of a better hypothesis that what I cut away from Hellman had life in it; that it 'escaped'; that it is now—well, trying to get at a thing like that, under the circumstances, I'd be inclined to say, we touch bottom!"

"Good God—the *motive!*" I almost whispered. "Why, it's horrible, Pelletier; it's positively uncanny. The Thing becomes, quite definitely, a horror. The motive—in that Thing! You're right, old man. Psychologically speaking, it 'touches bottom,' as you say."

"And humanly speaking," added Dr. Pelletier, in a very quiet voice.

Stephen came out and announced breakfast. It was one o'clock. We went in and ate rather silently. As Stephen was serving the dessert Dr. Pelletier spoke to him:

"Was Hellman's father a white man, do you happen to know, Stephen?"

"De man was an engineer on board an English trading vessel, sar."

"What about his mother?" probed the doctor.

"Her a resident of Antigua, sar," replied Stephen promptly, "and is yet alive. I am acquainted with her. Hellman ahlways send her some portion of his earnings, sar, very regularly. At de time Hellman born, her a 'ooman which do washing for ships' crews, an' make an excellent living. Nowadays, de poor soul liddle more than a piteous invalid, sar. Her ahlways a small liddle 'ooman, not too strong."

"I take it she is a dark woman?" remarked the doctor, smiling at Stephen.

Stephen, who is a medium brown young man, a 'Zambo," as they say in the English Islands like St. Kitts and Montserrat and Antigua, grinned broadly at this, displaying a set of magnificent, glistening teeth.

"Sar," he replied, "Hellman's mother de precisely identical hue of dis fella," and Stephen touched with his index finger the neat black bow-tie which set off the snowy whiteness of his immaculate drill houseman's jacket. Pelletier and I exchanged glances as we smiled at Stephen's little joke.

On the gallery immediately after lunch, over coffee, we came back to that bizarre topic which Dr. Pelletier had called the "motive." Considered quite apart from the weird aspect of attributing a motive to a quasi-human creature of the size of a rat, the matter was clear enough. The Thing had relentlessly attacked Brutus Hellman again and again, with an implacable fiendishness; its brutal, single-minded efforts being limited in their disastrous effects only by its diminutive size and relative deficiency of strength. Even so, it had succeeded in driving a full-grown man, its victim, into a condition not very far removed from imbecility.

What obscure processes had gone on piling up cumulatively to a fixed purpose of pure destruction in that primitive, degenerated organ that served the Thing for a brain! What dreadful weeks and months and years of semi-conscious brooding, of existence endured parasitically as an appendage upon the instinctively loathed body of the normal brother! What savage hatred had burned itself into that minute, distorted personality! What incalculable instincts, deep buried in the backgrounds of the black heredity through the mother, had come into play—as evidenced by the Thing's construction of the typical African hut as its habitation—once it had come, after the separation, into active consciousness, the new-born, freshly-realized freedom to exercise and release all that acrid, seething hatred upon him who had usurped its powers of self-expression, its very life itself! What manifold thwarted instincts had, by the processes of substitution, crystallized themselves into one overwhelming, driving desire—the consuming instinct for revenge!

I shuddered as all this clarified itself in my mind, as I formed, vaguely, some kind of mental image of that personality. Dr. Pelletier was speaking again. I forced my engrossed mind to listen to him. He seemed very grave and determined, I noticed.

"We must put an end to all this, Canevin," he was saying. "Yes, we must put an end to it."

Ever since that first Sunday evening when the attacks began, as I look back over that hectic period, it seems to me that I had had in mind primarily the idea of capture and destruction of what had crystallized in my mind as "The Thing." Now a new and totally bizarre idea came in to cause some mental conflict with the destruction element in that vague plan. This was the almost inescapable conviction that the Thing had been originally—whatever it might be properly named now—a human being.

As such, knowing well, as I did, the habits of the blacks of our Lesser Antilles, it had, unquestionably, been received into the church by the initial process of baptism. That indescribable creature which had been an appendage on Brutus Hellman's body, had been, was now, according to the teaching of the church, a Christian. The idea popped into my mind along with various other sidelights on the situation, stimulated into being by the discussion with Dr. Pelletier which I have just recorded.

The idea itself was distressing enough, to one who, like myself, have always kept up the teachings of my own childhood, who has never found it necessary, in these days of mental unrest, to doubt, still less to abandon, his religion. One of the concomitants of this idea was that the destruction of the Thing after its problematical capture, would be an awkward affair upon my conscience, for, however far departed the Thing had got from its original status as "A child of God—an inheritor of the Kingdom of Heaven," it must retain, in some obscure fashion, its human, indeed its Christian, standing. There are those, doubtless, who might well regard this scruple of mine as quite utterly ridiculous, who would lay all the stress on the plain necessity of stopping the Thing's destructive malignancy without reference to any such apparently far-fetched and artificial considerations. Nevertheless this aspect of our immediate problem, Pelletier's gravely enunciated dictum: "We must put an end to all this," weighed heavily on my burdened mind. It must be remembered that I had put in a dreadful week over the affair.

I mention this "scruple" of mine because it throws up into relief, in a sense, those events which followed very shortly after Dr. Pelletier had summed up what necessarily lay before us, in that phrase of his.

We sat on the gallery and cogitated ways and means, and it was in the midst of this discussion that the scruple alluded to occurred to me. I did not mention it to Pelletier. I mentally conceded, of course, the necessity of capture. The subsequent disposal of the Thing could wait on that.

We had pretty well decided, on the evidence, that the Thing had been lying low during the day in the little hut-like arrangement which it appeared to have built for itself. Its attacks so far had occurred only at night. If we were correct, the capture would be a comparatively simple affair. There was, as part of the equipment in my house, a small bait net, of the circular closing-in-from-the-bottom kind, used occasionally when I took guests on a deep-sea fishing excursion out to Congo or Levango Bays. This I unearthed, and looked over. It was intact, recently mended, without any holes in the tightly meshed netting designed to capture and retain small fish to be used later as live bait.

Armed with this, our simple plan readily in mind, we proceeded together to the alleyway about half-past two that afternoon, or, to be more precise, we were just at that moment starting down the gallery steps leading into my yard, when our ears were assailed by a succession of piercing, childish screams from the vicinity of the house's rear.

I rushed down the steps, four at a time, the more unwieldy Pelletier following me as closely as his propulsive apparatus would allow. I was in time to see, when I reached the corner of the house, nearly everything that was happening, almost from its beginning. It was a scene which, reproduced in a drawing accurately limned, would appear wholly comic. Little Aesculapius, the washer's small, black child, his eyes popping nearly from his head, his diminutive black legs twinkling under his single flying garment, his voice uttering blood-curdling yowls of pure terror, raced diagonally across the yard in the direction of his mother's washtub near the kitchen door, the very embodiment of crude, ungovernable fright, a veritable caricature, a figure of fun.

And behind him, coming on implacably, for all the world like a misshapen black frog, bounded the Thing, in hot pursuit, Its red tongue lolling out of Its gash of a mouth, Its diminutive blubbery lips drawn back in a wide snarl through which a murderous row of teeth flashed viciously in the pouring afternoon sunlight. Little Aesculapius was making good the promise of his relatively long, thin legs, fright driving him. He outdistanced the Thing hopelessly, yet It forged ahead in a rolling, leaping series of bounds, using hands and arms, frog-like, as well as Its strange, withered, yet strangely powerful bandied legs.

The sight, grotesque as it would have been to anyone unfamiliar with the Thing's history and identity, positively sickened me. My impulse was to cover my face with my hands, in the realization of its underlying horror. I could feel a faint nausea creeping over me, beginning to dim my senses. My washer-woman's screams had added to the confusion within a second or two after those of the child had begun, and now, as I hesitated in my course towards the scene of confusion, those of the cook and scullery-maid were added to the cacophonous din in my back yard. Little Aesculapius, his garment stiff against the breeze of his own progress, disappeared around the rear-most corner of the house to comparative safety through the open kitchen door. He had, as I learned sometime afterwards, been playing about the yard and had happened upon the little hut in its obscure and seldom-visited alleyway. He had stooped, and picked it up. "The Thing"—the child used that precise term to describe It—lay, curled up, asleep within. It had leaped to Its splayed feet with a snarl of rage, and gone straight for the little Negro's foot.

Thereafter the primitive instinct for self-preservation and Aesculapius' excellent footwork had solved his problem. He reached the kitchen door, around the corner and out of our sight, plunged within, and took immediate refuge atop the shelf of a kitchen cabinet well out of reach of that malignant, unheard-of demon like a big black frog which was pursuing him and which, doubtless, would haunt his dreams for the rest of his existence. So much for little Aesculapius, who thus happily passes out of the affair.

My halting was, of course, only momentary. I paused, as I have mentioned, but for so brief a period as not to allow Dr. Pelletier to catch up with me. I ran, then, with the net open in my hands, diagonally across the straight course being pursued by the Thing. My mind was made up to intercept It, entangle It in the meshes. This should not be difficult considering its smallness and the comparative shortness of Its arms and legs; and, having rendered It helpless, to face the ultimate problem of Its later disposal. But this plan of mine was abruptly interfered with. Precisely as the flying body of the pursued pick'ny disappeared around the corner of the house, my cook's cat, a ratter with a neighborhood reputation and now, although for the moment I failed to realize it, quite clearly an instrument of that Providence responsible for my "scruple," came upon the scene with violence, precision, and that uncanny accuracy which actuates the feline in all its physical manifestations.

This avatar, which, according to a long-established custom, had been sunning itself demurely on the edge of the rain-water piping which ran along the low eaves of the three yard cabins, aroused by the discordant yells of the child and the three women in four distinct keys, had arisen, taken a brief, preliminary stretch, and condescended to turn its head towards the scene below. . . .

The momentum of the cat's leap arrested instantaneously the Thing's course of pursuit, bore it, sprawled out and flattened, to the ground, and twenty sharp powerful retractile claws sank simultaneously into the prone little body.

The Thing never moved again. A more merciful snuffing out would be difficult to imagine.

It was a matter of no difficulty to drive Junius, the cat, away from his kill. I am on terms of pleasant intimacy with Junius. He allowed me to take the now limp and flaccid little body away from him quite without protest, and sat down where he was, licking his paws and readjusting his rumpled fur.

And thus, unexpectedly, without intervention on our part, Pelletier and I saw brought to its sudden end, the tragical denouement of what seems to me to be one of the most outlandish and most distressing affairs which could ever have been evolved out of the mad mentality of Satan, who dwells in his own place to distress the children of men.

And that night, under a flagstone in the alleyway, quite near where the Thing's strange habitation had been taken up, I buried the mangled leathery little body of that unspeakably grotesque homunculus which had once been the twin brother of my houseman, Brutus Hellman. In consideration of my own scruple which I have mentioned, and because, in all probability, this handful of strange material which I lowered gently into its last resting-place had once been a Christian, I repeated the Prayer of Committal from the Book of Common Prayer. It may have been— doubtless was, in one sense—a grotesque act on my part. But I cherish the conviction that I did what was right.

BLACK TANCRÈDE

IT IS TRUE that Black Tancrède did not curse Hans De Groot as his mangled body collapsed on the rack, and that he did curse Gardelin. But, it must be remembered, Governor Gardelin went home, to Denmark, and so escaped—whatever it was that happened to Achilles Mendoza and Julius Mohrs; and Black Tancrède, who always kept his word, they said, had cursed three!

The Grand Hotel of St. Thomas in the Virgin Islands glistens in the almost intolerable brilliance of the Caribbean sunlight, because that great edifice is whitewashed in every corner, every winter. Built somewhat more than a century ago, it is a noble example of that tropical architecture which depends, for its style, upon the structural necessity for resistance to summer hurricanes. Its massive walls of stone, brick, and heavy cement are thick and ponderous. The ceilings of its huge, square rooms are eighteen feet high. Despite its solidity, the 1916 hurricane took the top story off the main building and this has never been replaced. The fact that the hotel is now uniformly a two-story structure somewhat mars its original symmetry, but it is still as impressive as in the days when the Danish Colonial High Court sat in one of its sections; when its "slave-pens" were especially noted for their safety.

Built alongside the great courtyard which its bulk surrounds, and toward the harbor, once the crater of a volcano in that era when Atlantis and its companion continent, Antillea, reared their proud civilizations in the central Atlantic, stand two houses, added, it is believed, some time after the construction of the original building. On this point the St. Thomas wiseacres continue to dispute. Nevertheless, under the house nearest to the hotel, and built with connecting steps leading to its great gallery, are those very slave-pens, converted nowadays into one enormous workroom where the hotel washing and ironing goes on, remorselessly, all the year round. During its early history, the hotel was called "Hotel du Commerce."

In that nearer, and slightly smaller of the two houses, I was installed for the winter. I took this house because I was accompanied that winter by Stephen de Lesseps, my young cousin, a boy of fourteen. Stephen's parents (his mother is my cousin Marie de Lesseps) had persuaded me to take him with me for the change of climate. Stephen is an agreeable young fellow. I gave him daily "lessons" and he read much himself, so that his education out of books was not neglected, and that major portion derived otherwise was enhanced. Stephen turned out on close association to be so manly, sensible, and generally companionable, that I congratulated myself upon yielding to my cousin Marie's suggestion.

In the middle of that winter, Marie and her sister Suzanne paid us a visit of a month. Mr. Joseph Reynolds, the American proprietor of the Grand Hotel, assigned them Room 4, a huge, double room, opening off the enormous hotel ballroom in which the major social functions of the Virgin Island capital are usually held. I am obliged to mention this background for the extraordinary story I have to tell. If I had not had Stephen along, I should not have remained in St. Thomas. I did so on his account. The capital, rather than my beloved island of Santa Cruz, was a better place for his education. Don Pablo Salazar, a famous teacher of Spanish, is resident there; the director of education lived in the neighboring house—there were many reasons.

And, if I had not had Stephen with me, Marie and Suzanne would not have made that visit, and so could not have spent a month in Number 4, and so this tale would never, perhaps, have been told.

The ladies arrived early in January, after a sweeping tour of "the lower islands"—those historic sea-jewels where England and France fought out the supremacy of the seas a century ago. They were delighted with Number 4. They slept on vast mahogany four-posters; they were entertained by everybody; they patronized St. Thomas' alluring shops; they reveled in the midsummer warmth of midwinter in this climate of balm and spice; they exclaimed over Stephen's growth and rejoiced over the fine edge with which one of the world's politest communities had ornamented the boy's naturally excellent manners. In brief, my lady cousins enjoyed their month tremendously and went home enthusiastic over the quaint charm and magnificent hospitality of the capital of the Virgin Islands, our Uncle Sam's most recent colonial acquisition, once the historic Danish West Indies.

Only one fly, it appeared, had agitated the ointment of their enjoyment. Neither, they eventually reported, could get proper sleep in Number 4 in spite of its airiness, its splendid beds, and its conveniences. At night, one or the other, and, as I learned later, sometimes both simultaneously, would be awakened out of refreshing sleep at that most unpropitious of all night hours, four o'clock in the morning.

They said very little of this to me. I found out later that they were extremely chary of admitting that anything whatever had been interfering with their enjoyment of my hospitality. But later, after they were gone, I did recall that Suzanne had mentioned, though lightly, how she had heard knocks at the double-doors of their big room, just at that hour. It had made little impression upon me at the time.

Long afterward, questioning them, I discovered that they had been awakened nearly every morning by the same thing! They had mentioned it to their room-maid, a black girl, who had appeared "stupid" about it; had only rolled her eyes, Marie said. They tried several explanations—brooms carelessly handled in the early morning; a permanent early "call" for some guest, perhaps an officer of marines who had to get to his duties very early. They rejected both those theories, and finally settled down to the explanation that some pious fellow-guest was accustomed to attend the earliest religious service of the day, which, in both the Anglican and Roman Catholic churches in St. Thomas, is at five in the morning. They knew, because they had several tunes answered the knocks, that there was never anybody at the door when they opened it. They reconciled their ultimate explanation with the discrepancy that the knocks were on their door, by the supposition that there was involved some strange, auditory illusion.

As I have said, these ladies were fascinated with St. Thomas, and they did not allow one minor disturbing element to interfere with their enjoyment of its many strange sights; the weird speech of the blacks; the magnificent hospitality; the Old World furniture; the street lamps; the delightful little vistas; the Caribbean's incredible indigo; especially, I think, with the many strange tales which they heard more or less incidentally.

For St. Thomas, the very home and heart of old romance, is full of strange tales. Here, in September, 1824, the pirate Fawcett with his two mates was publicly hanged. To this very day, great steel doors guard most St. Thomas stores, and particularly the funds of the Dansk Vestindiske Nationalbank, from marauders, as anciently those same doors guarded them from the frequent raids of the buccaneers. St. Thomas' streets have more than once run red with human blood; for, like Panama, it is a town which has been sacked, though never burned like Frederiksted on the neighboring island of Santa Cruz.

Among these many tales was that of Black Tancrède. This negro, a Dahomeyan, so said tradition, had lived for a while in one of those very slave-pens under my house. He had been, strangely enough, a Haitian refugee, although a full-blooded black African. Many Caucasian refugees from Haiti had come to St Thomas In the days of Dessalines, Toussaint l'Ouverture, and Henry Cristophe, the black king of Northwestern Haiti, the bloody days of that wise despot whose marvelous citadel still towers incredibly on the hills behind Cap Haitien and who is chiefly remembered for his tyrannies, but who is probably the only person who ever made millions out of the "free" labor of his fellow blacks!

Tancrède had, so said tradition, incurred the enmity of Cristophe, and that in the days of his power was a fearsome thing for any man. But, unlike other known unfortunates who had risked that terrible anger, Tancrède had escaped Cristophe's executioner. That personage boasted that he had had so much practise with the broadsword that he could remove a head without soiling the victim's collar!

By some hook or crook, hidden probably in the stinking, rat-infested hold of some early Nineteenth Century sailing-vessel, perhaps buried under goathides or bales of *bacalhao,* Tancrède had shivered and sweated his way to the Danish refuge of St. Thomas. There he fell swiftly into inescapable debt, for he was a fighting-man from a warlike tribe, and no bargainer. Therefore he had become the property of one Julius Mohrs, and because of that his connection with the old hotel had begun. Black Tancrède had been lodged, for safekeeping, in one of those same slave-pens under my house. He had soon escaped from that servitude, for his strong, bitter soul could not brook it, and made his way to the neighboring Danish island of St. Jan. There he is next heard of as a "free laborer" on the sugar estates of Erasmus Espersen. In the "Rising" of 1833 he was prominent as a leader of those who revolted against the harsh laws of Governor Gardelin. Later, whether by the French troops from Martinique who came in to help the Danes put down their Slave War, or by the Spanish troops from Porto Rico, Black Tancrède had been captured alive, which was a grave error of judgment on his part, and brought back to St. Thomas in chains, there to be tortured to death.

That sentence was delivered in the Danish colonial high court, sitting in its own quarters in the hotel, by Governor Gardelin's judge.

First Black Tancrède's hands had been cut off, one a day. Then he suffered the crushing of his feet (after "three pinches with a hot iron instrument"), a punishment consummated with a heavy bar of iron in the hands of Achilles Mendoza, the executioner, himself a black slave. The iron sheared through his leg-bones, and he was "pinched," and his hands chopped off, because he had been so unfortunate as to be caught in insurrection, bearing weapons, and he was therefore to be made an example by a governor whose name is even now execrated among the black people.

With his last expiring breath Black Tancrède cursed his tormentors. He cursed Achilles Mendoza. He cursed Julius Mohrs. He cursed Governor Gardelin. They buried his shattered body in quicklime in the courtyard of the fort, and with it went his left hand, which was clutched so firmly about the wooden crossbar of the rack that it could not be pried loose. Mendoza therefore broke off the crossbar with the hand attached, and threw it into the limepit. The other hand, chopped off the day before, had disappeared, and no effort was made to recover it. Such items in those "good old days" were not infrequently picked up and kept by onlookers as interesting souvenirs.

Four months after the execution, Julius Mohrs was found strangled in bed one morning. Even the lash failed to elicit any testimony from his household. No one has ever known who committed that murder. Mohrs, like Governor Gardelin, had the reputation of being harsh with slaves.

Achilles Mendoza died "of a fit" in the year 1835, in the open air. He was, in fact, crossing the courtyard of the hotel at the time and was not more than a few steps from the doors leading into the slave-pens. Many bystanders saw him fall, although it was at night, for the full moon of the Caribbee Islands—by whose light I have myself read print—was shining overhead. Indeed, so much light comes from the Caribbean moon that illuminates these latitudes—degree seventeen runs through Santa Cruz, eighteen through St. Thomas—that on full moonlight nights in the "good old days," the capital itself saved the cost of street-lights; and that is the custom even today in the Santa Crucian towns.

Some of the black people at first believed that Mendoza had strangled himself! This foolish idea was doubtless derived from the fact that both the executioner's hands had gone to his throat even before he fell, gasping and foaming at the mouth, and they were found clasped unbreakably together, the great muscles of his mighty arms rigid in death with the effort, when his now worthless body was unceremoniously gathered up and carted away for early morning burial.

Naturally, everybody who remembered Black Tancrède and his curses, and his character—that is, everybody who believed in black magic as well as in Black Tancrède-was certain that that malefactor, murderer, leader of revolt, consummated a posthumous revenge. Perhaps Julius Mohrs, too—

The Danes pooh-poohed this solution of the two unaccountable deaths in the capital of their West Indian colony, but that did not affect black belief in the slightest degree. Black Quashee was in those days only a generation removed from Black Africa, where such matters are commonplaces. Such beliefs, and the practises which accompany them, had come in through Cartagena and other routes, deviously and direct, into the West Indies from the Gold Coast, from Dahomey and Ashantee and the Bight of Benin—all the way, indeed, from Dakar to the Congo mouth regions—into the West Indies indeed, where Quashee's sheer fecundity, now that the "good old days" are no more, and Quashee is a Christian of one kind or another, and often a high school or even a college graduate, has caused him vastly to outnumber his erstwhile white masters. White people are now Quashee's masters no longer, though they still live beside him in the West Indies, in a constantly diminishing proportion, under that same bright moon, that same glowing sun, in the shade of the mighty tamarinds, beside the eye-scorching scarlet of the hibiscus, the glaring purple and magenta of the bougainvillea.

Governor Gardelin returned to Denmark very soon after the Slave War of 1883, where, so far as one may know from perusal of the old records, he died in his bed full of years and honors.

As I have mentioned, my cousins, Marie and Suzanne, returned to the continental United States. They left about the tenth of February, and Stephen and I, regretting their departure, settled down for the rest of that winter, planning to return the middle of May.

One morning, a few weeks after their departure, Reynolds, the proprietor, asked me a question.

"Did you hear the uproar last night, or, rather, early this morning?"

"No," said I. "What was 'the uproar'? If it was out in the streets I might have heard it, but if it happened inside the hotel, my house is so detached that I should probably have heard nothing of it and gone right on sleeping."

"It was inside," said Reynolds, "so you probably wouldn't have noticed it. The servants are all chattering about it this morning, though. They believe it is another manifestation of the Jumbee in Number 4. By the way, Mr. Canevin, your cousins were in that room. Did they ever mention any disturbance to you?"

"Why, yes, now that you speak of it. My cousin Suzanne spoke of somebody knocking on their door; about four in the morning I believe it happened. I think it happened more than once. They imagined it was somebody being 'called' very early, and the servant knocking on the wrong door or something of that kind. They didn't say much about it to me. What is 'the Jumbee in Number 4?' That intrigues me. I never happened to hear that one!"

Now a "Jumbee" is, of course, a West Indian ghost. In the French islands the word is "Zombi." Jumbees have various characteristics, which I will not pause to enumerate, but one of these is that a Jumbee is always black. White persons, apparently, do not "walk" after death, although I have personally known three white gentlemen planters who were believed to be werewolves! Among the West Indian black population occurs every belief, every imaginable practise of the occult, which is interwoven closely into their lives and thoughts; everything from mere "charms" to active necromancy; from the use of the deadly *Vaudoux* to the "toof from a dead," which last renders a gambler lucky! Jumbee is a generic word. It means virtually any kind of a ghost, apparition, or *revenant*. I was not in the least surprized to learn that Number 4,

Grand Hotel, had its other-worldly attendant. My sole ground for wonder was that I had not heard of it before now! Now that I recalled the matter, something had disturbed Marie and Suzanne in that room. "Tell me about it, please, Mr. Reynolds," I requested.

Mr. Reynolds smiled. He is a man of education and he, too, knows his West Indies.

"In this case it is only a general belief," he answered. "The only specific information about 'the Jumbee in Number 4' is that it wakes occupants up early in the morning. There has, it seems, 'always been a Jumbee' connected with the room. I daresay the very frying-pans in the kitchen have their particular Jumbees, if they happen to be old enough! That rumpus this morning was only that we had a tourist, a Mr. Ledwith, staying over-night—came over from Porto Rico in the *Catherine* and left this morning for 'down the islands' on the *Dominica*. He came in pretty late last night from a party with friends in the town. He explained later that he couldn't sleep because of somebody knocking on his door. He called out several times, got no answer; the knocking went on, and then he lost his temper. He reached out of bed and picked up the earthenware water-jug. His aim was excellent, even though he may have had a drop too much at his party. He hit the door-handle, smashed the jug into fragments, and then, really aroused, got up, flung open the door, found nobody there, and took it into his head that somebody was having a joke on him. Absurd! The man was a total stranger to everybody in the hotel. "He raged around the ballroom and woke up the Gilbertsons and Mrs. Peck—you know they have rooms on that side—and at last he awakened me and I got up and persuaded him to go back to bed. He said there were no more knocks after that. I was afraid it might have disturbed you and Stephen. I'm glad it didn't. Of course such a rumpus is very unusual in the hotel at any time."

"Hm," said I, "well, well!" I had been thinking while Mr. Reynolds made this long speech about the nocturnal activities of the unknown Mr. Ledwith. I could not talk with him. He had already sailed that morning.

I was really intrigued by now—that occurrence coupled with the experience of my cousins! Of course I knew very little about that, for they had said almost nothing. But it was enough to arouse my interest in "the Jumbee in Number 4."

That was the only time Mr. Reynolds and I spoke of the matter, and for some time, although I kept my ears open, I heard nothing further about Number 4. When the "trouble" did start up again, I was in Number 4 myself. That came about in this manner.

An American family named Barnes, permanent residents of St. Thomas—I believe Barnes was a minor official of the public works or the agricultural department of the Virgin Island government—let their house-lease expire and decided to move into the hotel at family-rates-by-the-month for the convenience. Mrs. Barnes had two young children, and was tired of household cares. She had employed, I think, some rather inferior servants, which always mean a heavy burden in the West Indies. One of the two hotel houses would suit them exactly. The other was occupied, by the year, by the director of education and his family, delightful Americans.

It was the first of May, and as Stephen and I were booked to sail on the twelfth for New York, I proposed to Mr. Reynolds that we give up our house to Mr. and Mrs. Barnes, and he could put us into one of the huge double rooms for the remainder of our stay. Mr. Reynolds put us into Number 4, probably the best of all the rooms, and which was, fortunately, vacant at the moment.

It happened that on our first night in our new quarters, I was out very late. I had gone, with the colonel in command of the naval station marines and his wife, to meet an incoming ship on which a certain Major Upton was returning to St. Thomas from a month's leave. Two days before the arrival of the ship, a cable had informed the colonel of Mrs. Upton's sudden death in Virginia. We did not know whether or not Upton had learned of his unexpected bereavement by wireless aboard ship, and we rather thought he had not. The ship was reported due at one a.m. She came in a little after two, and after meeting Upton—who had, fortunately, received a wireless—and making his arrival as pleasant as we could for him under the circumstances, I got back to the hotel about three-thirty in the morning.

I came in at the side door, which is always open, walked softly along the great length of the ballroom, and very quietly opened the door of Number 4. By the streaming moonlight which was pouring in through the open jalousies of the great room, I could see Stephen's outlines, dimly, through the cloud of mosquito-netting which covered his enormous four-poster. I undressed silently, so that I should not disturb my young cousin. I was just ready to turn in, my soiled drill clothes in the washbag, my white buckskin shoes neatly treed, my other things laid away where they belonged—for I am a rather fussy fellow about such matters—and it was within a minute or two to four o'clock in the morning; I know I was beastly tired; when, just beside me, on the door leading in from the ballroom, came an abrupt, unmistakable rap-rap-rap! There could be no possible doubt about it. I was standing within three feet of the door at the moment the raps were delivered. I, Gerald Canevin, am a teller of the truth. I admit that I felt the cold chills which are characteristic of sudden, almost uncontrollable, paralyzing fear, run swiftly up and down my spine; that acute prickling at the hair roots which is called one's "hair standing on end."

But, if Gerald Canevin is a trifle old-maidish about the arrangement of his personal belongings, and, even damagingly, truthful, he may boast, and justly, that no man living can call him a poltroon.

I took one firm step to that door and flung it open, and—so help me God!—as I turned the small, old-fashioned brass knob, the last of the raps—for the summons was repeated, just as the convivial Ledwith had alleged—sounded within three inches of my hand, on the other side of the door.

The great-ghostly still ballroom stood silent and empty. Not a sound, not a movement disturbed its early-morning, dead, serene emptiness. I raked the room with my scrutiny. Everything was visible because the vivid moonlight-the moon had been full two nights before—came flooding in from the gallery with its nine Moorish arches, overlooking the harbor.

There was nothing—absolutely, literally, nothing—to be seen or heard. I glanced back over my shoulder along the wall through which the door of Number 4 opens. What was that? I could feel my heart skip a beat, then start pounding. A dim something, the merest shadowy outline, it seemed, in the form of a gigantic negro was moving along the wall toward the passageway, curtained from the ballroom, which leads to the main entrance of the hotel below.

Even as I looked, the strange form seemed to melt and vanish, and there came a hard, dull thud from the direction where I imagined I had seen it slipping furtively along the wall.

I looked narrowly, my heart still pounding, and there, on the floor moving rapidly from me in the same direction I had imagined that sinister figure following, and with a queer, awkward movement suggestive of a crab's sidelong gait, but moving in utter silence, there ran along the bare floor something about the size of a baseball.

I was barefooted and in thin, China-silk pajamas, but I started, weaponless, after the thing. It was, I surmised, the biggest tarantula I had ever seen in or out of the West Indies. Certainly it was no crab, although its size and even its gait would suggest one of our boxlike, compact land-crabs. But a crab, running away like that, would make a distinctive, identifying, hard rattle with its shell-covered feet on that hard, wooden floor, and this thing ran silently, like velvet.

What I should do with, or to, the tarantula if I caught it, I did not stop to consider. I suppose it was a kind of instinct that sent me in pursuit. I gained on it, but it slipped past the curtains ahead of me and was lost to sight in the broad passageway on the other side of the stairs' head. As soon as I had passed the curtain I saw that any attempt to catch the thing would be an impossibility. There would be innumerable hiding-places; the main entrance doors were closed tight down below there, and the stair-well was as dark as the inside of Jonah's whale.

I turned back, perforce, and re-entered Number 4, shut the door quietly behind me, and turned in upon my own gigantic four-poster and tucked the mosquito-netting under the edge of the mattress. I slept at once and did not awaken until five and one-half hours later, at nine-thirty in the morning. The excellent Stephen, realizing the situation, had repaid my pussyfooting in his interest of the earlier morning by getting dressed in silence and ordering my breakfast sent in at this hour.

That was Saturday morning, and there were no lessons for Stephen. I took advantage of that fact to put in a very much occupied day at my typewriter, and I got such a start on what I was then engaged in writing that I determined, if possible, to finish it the next day in time for the New York mail which goes out through Porto Rico every week. A brief, unaccustomed siesta Saturday afternoon helped make up for some lack of sleep. I decided to get up and go to that horribly "early" service at five on Sunday morning. That would give me a reason for early rising—which I have always secretly abominated!—and a good day's start. Stephen and I retired that evening as soon as he returned from his moving-pictures at the naval station; that was about nine-thirty.

I must have grown wearier than I had realized, sitting up for Major Upton's ship, and accompanying him to the colonel's quarters afterward; for I slept like the dead, and had my usual fight with myself to get up and shut off an insistent alarm-clock at four-fifteen. I got to church in time, and was back again a few minutes before six. It was barely dawn when I came in at the side entrance and up the stairs.

As I walked along the still dim ballroom toward Number 4, the tarantula, or land-crab, or whatever the thing might prove to be, came sidling in that same awkward fashion which I had noted along the edge of the sidewall, toward me this time. It was as though the creature were returning from the hiding-place whither I had chased him Saturday morning.

I was carrying a tough, resilient walking-stick, of native black wattle, cut by myself on Estate Ham's Bay, over on Santa Cruz, two years before. I stepped faster toward the oncoming thing, with this stick poised in my hand. I saw now in the rapidly brightening dawn what was wrong with the spider—it was obvious now that it was no landcrab. The thing was maimed. It had, apparently, lost several of its legs, and so proceeded in that odd, crablike fashion which I had noted before. A spider should have eight legs, as most people know. This one came hunching and sidling along on five or six.

The thing, moving rapidly despite its paucity of legs, was almost at the door to Number 4. I ran toward it, for the door stood slightly open, and I did not want that horrible creature to go into my room on account of Stephen. I struck at it, viciously, but it eluded my black wattle and slipped in under the conch-shell which served as a door-chock.

Conches have many uses in the West Indies. In the Bahamas their contents serve as a food-staple. They occasionally yield "pearls," which have some value to jewelers. One sees the shells everywhere—bordering garden paths, outlining cemetery plots, built, with cement, into ornamental courses like shining pink bricks. In the Grand Hotel every door has a conch for a chock. The one at my door was a very old one, painted, in a dark brown color, to preserve it from disintegration due to the strong, salt air.

I approached the shell, now covering the huge tarantula, with some caution. The bite of our native tarantulas in St. Thomas is rarely or never fatal, but it can put the human victim into the hospital for several days, and this fellow, as I have said, was the largest I had ever seen, in or out of St. Thomas. I poked the end of my stick under the lip-edge of the shell, and turned it suddenly over. The spider had disappeared. Obviously it had crawled inside the shell. There is a lot of room inside a good-sized conch. I decided to take a chance. I did not want that thing about the place, certainly.

Keeping my eye on the upturned shell, I stepped over to the center of the ballroom and picked up a week-old Sunday supplement rotogravure section of one of the New York newspapers, crumpled it, folded it into a kind of wad, and with this, very gingerly—for the tarantula is a fighter and no timid beast—effectually stopped up the long triangular entrance to the shell's inside. Then, picking it up, I carried it outside onto the stone-flagged gallery.

Here things were appreciably lighter. The dawn was brightening into the tropic day every instant, and I could now see everything clearly.

I raised the conch-shell and brought it down crashing on the tessellated floor.

As I had expected, the old shell smashed into many fragments, and I stood by, my black wattle raised and ready to strike at the tarantula as it attempted to run away. I had figured, not unnaturally, that the experience of having its rocklike refuge suddenly picked up, carried away, and then crashing to pieces about itself, would, from the tarantula's viewpoint, prove at least momentarily disconcerting, and I should have a chance to slay the loathsome thing at my leisure. But, to my surprize, nothing ran out of the shattered shell.

I bent and looked closer. The fragments were relatively both large and small, from powdery dust all the way to a few chunks as big as my two fists. I poked at one of these, of an extraordinary and arresting shape, a strangely suggestive shape, though colored a dirty pink like the rest of the conch's lining. I turned it over with the end of my stick.

It was the hand of a negro, which, lying palm upward, had at first seemed pink. The palm of the hand of the blackest of black Africans is pink So is the sole of the foot But there was no mistaking the back of that sooty, claw-like thing. It was a severed hand, and it had originally grown upon an owner who had no admixture of any blood other than that of Africa. The name "Tancrède" leapt to my mind. Had he not, even among his fellow slaves, been called "Black Tancrède"? He had, and my knowledge of that ancient tale and the sooty duskiness of this ancient relic conspired forthwith to cause me to leap to that outrageous, that incredible conclusion. The hand of Black Tancrède—this was a right hand, and so, said tradition, was the one which had first been severed and then disappeared—or, at least, the veritable hand of some intensely dark negro, lay there before me on the gallery floor, among the debris of an ancient conch-shell.

I drew a deep breath, for it was an unsettling experience, stooped, and picked the thing up. It was as dry and hard as so much conch-shell, and surprizingly heavy. I looked at it carefully, turning it about and examining it thoroughly; for I was alone on the gallery. Nobody was stirring in the hotel; even the kitchen was silent.

I slipped the hand into the pocket of my drill jacket, and returned to Number 4. I laid the hand down on the marble-topped table which stands in the room's center, and looked at it. Stephen, I had noted at once, was absent. He had got up, and was now, doubtless, in his shower-bath.

I had not been looking at it very long, before an explanation, too far-fetched to be dwelt upon or even to be seriously entertained, was invading my dazed mind. Something on five or six "legs" had run under that conch-shell. Nothing, save this, had been there when I smashed the shell. There were the surface facts, and I was my own witness. There was no hearsay about it. This was no black Quashee tale of marvels and wonderment.

I heard a pad-pad outside, like slippered feet, and I had the thing in my pocket again when Stephen came in, glowing from his shower. I did not want to explain that hand to the boy.

"Good morning, Cousin Gerald," said Stephen. "You got off early, didn't you? I heard your alarm-clock but I turned over and went to sleep again."

"Yes," I answered. "You see, I have a lot of work to get through with today."

"I'd have gone with you," continued Stephen, half-way into his fresh clothes by now, "if you'd waked me up! I'm going to six o'clock church if I can make it."

He dressed rapidly, and with another pleasant, hasty word or two, the boy was off, running. The "English Church" is quite near by.

I got up, left Number 4 empty, crossed the ballroom diagonally, and entered Mr. Reynolds' sanctum at its western extremity. I had thought of something. I must do what I could to clear up, or put away forever, if possible, that explanation, the details of which were invading my excited mind, pressing into it remorselessly.

I went to the lowest shelf of one of his bookcases, and took out the three heavy, calf-bound, ancient registers of the Hotel du Commerce. I must find out, on the off-chance that the room numbers had not been changed since then, who had occupied Room 4 at the time of Black Tancrède's execution and cursings. That, for the moment, seemed to me absolutely the salient fact, the key to the whole situation.

I could hardly believe my eyes when the faded entry, the ink brown, the handwriting oddly curlicued, jumped out at me.

For all of the year 1832, 1833, and most of 1834 besides, Room 4, Hotel du Commerce, Raoul Patit, proprietor, had been occupied by one Hans de Groot. Hans de Groot had been Governor Gardelin's judge of the Danish Colonial high court. Hans de Grout had condemned Black Tancrède to death, by amputation of hands, pinching, and breaking on the rack.

I had my explanation.

If only this were a romance, I should proceed to tell how thereafter I had applied, in the traditional method for the laying of this kind of ghost—a ghost with an unfulfilled desire, promise, or curse—how I had applied for permission to restore the hand to the resting-place of Black Tancrède. I should recite the examination of old records, the location of the lime-pit in the Fort yard; I might even have the horrible thing which lay in my jacket pocket "escape" to wreak devastation upon me after unavailing efforts on my part to avoid destruction; a final twist of luck, the destruction of the hand.

But this is not romance, and I am not attempting to make "quite a tale" of these sober facts.

What I did was to proceed straight to the hotel kitchen, where fat Lucinda the cook was cutting breakfast bacon at a table, and two dusky assistants preparing grapefruit and orange-juice against the hour for breakfast.

"Good morning, Lucinda," I began; "is your fire going?"

"Marnin', Mars' Canevin, sar, returned Lucinda, "hot, good'n hot, sar. Is you' desirous to cook someting?"

Both handmaidens giggled at this, and I smiled with them.

"I only have something I wish to burn," said I, explaining my early-morning visit.

I approached the glowing stove, anticipating Lucinda, and waving her back to her bacon-cutting, lifted a lid, and dropped the horrible, mummified thing into the very heart of a bed of cherry-colored coals.

It twisted in the heat, as though alive and protesting. It gave off a faint, strange odor of burning, like very old leather. But within a few moments the dry and brittle skin and the calcined bones were only scraps of shapeless, glowing embers.

I replaced the stovelid. I was satisfied. I would now satisfy Lucinda, if not her very natural curiosity. I handed her with an engaging smile one of the small, brown, five-franc currency bills which are still issued by the Dansk Vestindiske Nationalbank, and are legal tender In our Uncle Sam's Virgin Islands.

"May t'anks, sar; Gahd bless yo', Mars' Canevin, sar," muttered the delighted Lucinda.

I nodded to them and walked out of the kitchen reasonably certain that the Jumbee of Number 4 would trouble guests no more at four o'clock in the morning, nor at any other hour; that eternity had now swallowed Black Tancrède, who tradition alleged, was a very persevering man and always kept his word. . . .

It is true, as I remarked at the beginning of this narrative, that Black Tancrède did not curse Hans de Groot, but that Governor Cardelin went home to Denmark and so escaped—whatever it was that happened to Achilles Mendoza and Julius Mohrs. Perhaps the persevering shade of Black Tancrède was limited, in the scope of its revengeful "projection" through that severed hand, to the island on which he died. I do not know, although there are almost fixed rules for these things; rules in which Quashee believes religiously.

But, since that morning, I, truthful Gerald Canevin, confess, I have never seen any large spider without at least an internal shudder. I can understand, I think, what that strange mental aberration called "spider fear" is like.

For I saw that thing which ran along the floor of the Grand Hotel ballroom like a maimed spider—I saw it go under that conch-shell. And it did not come out as it went in.

With more of gentleness he laid again his hand on the delicate, rounded shoulder. As gently he turned the girl about and marched her, resolutely—like a Dane—toward the gallery steps. His fastidiousness had reasserted itself.

"Good night—my child," said Cornelis.

The girl looked up at him shyly, out of the corners of her eyes, puzzled and resentful.

"Good night, sar," she murmured, and slipped down the steps and like a shadow around the corner of the house.

Cornelis walked firmly into his house and shut the door behind him. He went into his dining-room and poured himself a glass of French brandy and rinsed out the glass from the earthenware water-gugglet, throwing the water onto the stone floor. Then he mounted the stairs to his bedroom, got into bed, rolled over on his side, and went to sleep.

On the morning after his tea he was riding about his fields so early that he was finished with his managerial inspection before nine. Ten o'clock saw him, very carefully shaved, and wearing spotless white drill and his best Danish straw hat instead of a sun helmet, driving a pair of horses in the light phaeton toward Christiansted.

That same afternoon, during the period devoted to swizzels of old rum or brandy and, especially among the Danes, tea and coffee and cakes—the period of sociability before the company at the various great houses broke up before its various dinner- parties—Cornelis called at the Nybladhs'. The Administrator and his wife were pleased to see him, as always. Several others were present, quite a company in fact, for the swizzel-hour at Nybladhs' was almost an official occasion.

After a quarter of an hour, Cornelis drew the Administrator aside and they spoke together briefly, then returned to the company gathered about an enormous mahogany table which held the silver swizzel jug and the afternoon's lunch.

At the next pause in the conversation Nybladh rose, focusing his guests' attention upon himself. He held up his glass.

"Be pleased to fill all glasses," he commanded, importantly.

There was a considerable bustle about the great round table. Nybladh noted the fulfilling of his command. Servants hurried about among the guests. When all were freshly served he cleared his throat and waved his own glass ceremoniously.

"I announce"—he paused, impressively, all eyes dutifully upon him. "I announce—the engagement of Herr Hansen and Miss Honoria Macartney. Skoal!" He boomed it out sonorously. Every glass was raised.

Cornelis bowed from the waist, deeply, to each of his pledgers, as they drank the health of himself and his bride-to-be.

Thus did Honoria, daughter of the great Irish-West Indian family of the Fighting Macartneys, become Fru Hansen, after an exceptionally brief engagement, and leave her father's house to live at Estate Fairfield with her husband who was the nephew of Old Strach.

A West Indian family does not pick up titles from populace by knocking about their estates and doing nothing. The Fighting Macartneys were well worthy of theirs. Even Saul Macartney, their ancient black sheep. who had paid the penalty of piracy by hanging in St. Thomas in 1824 along with the notorious Fawcett, his chief, and who, as some believed, had been strangely magicked even after his death by his cousin Camilla Lanigan who was believed to practise obeah and was immensely respected by the negroes—even the disgraced Saul was no poltroon. The jewels Saul and Captain Fawcett buried under Melbourne House, Saul's Santa Cruz mansion, had not been handed that miscreant over the counter!

This young Honoria was of that sanguine blood, even though her sheltered life had made her walk somewhat mincingly and there was no color in her cheeks. She began her reign at Fairfield like a sensible young housewife, studying Cornelis' likes and dislikes, satisfying him profoundly, beyond his very moderate expectations. The ardent yet self-contained young man had linked to himself something compounded of fire and silk. Honoria brought to her housekeeping, too, great skill and knowledge, from her young lifetime in her mother's great house near Christiansted.

She was a jewel of a wife, this young Honoria Hansen, born Macartney. Cornelis came suddenly to love her with an ardency which even he had never dreamed of as possible, like flame. Then their love was tempered in a fearful happening.

One morning when Cornelis was riding early about his sugar fields, it came to him, traversing a cane-range on his black mare, Aase, that never, before or since that sleepless night when he had called the girl to him on the gallery, had he laid eyes upon that girl. That he would recognize the girl whom, for a moment of abandoned forgetfulness of his fastidious reserve, he had held in his arms, whose body had lain against his heart, was beyond question in his mind. Then it occurred to him that he had thought of the girl as living in his village. That night when he had dismissed her, she had walked away around the house toward the cabins at the rear. He shuddered—those cabins!

Yet the fact remained that, cogitate the matter as he might, riding along at Aase's delicate walking pace, he could not recollect having laid eyes upon her, either before or since that night when he had sent her away. It was very curious, inexplicable indeed—if the girl lived in his village. There was really no way to inquire. Well, it did not greatly matter, of course! A brown girl was—a brown girl. They were all alike. Cornelis rode on to another cane-field.

Telepathy, perhaps! When he arrived at Fairfield House toward eleven under the mounting brilliance of the late-morning sunlight, and tossed his bridle-reins to Alonzo his groom at the front gallery steps, the girl stood beside the door of Fairfield House, inside the high hallway. She curtsied gravely to him as he passed within.

Cornelis' mouth went dry. He managed to nod at the girl, who reached for his sun helmet and hung it on the hallway hatrack.

"Mistress say de brekfuss prepare' in few moments, sar," announced the girl.

Honoria, in his absence, it appeared, had engaged this girl as a house servant. There was no other explanation of her presence in the house. She had been carefully dressed, rustling with starch, the very picture of demureness. Cornelis strode upstairs to wash before late breakfast, which came at eleven.

His equanimity was sufficiently restored after breakfast to enquire of Honoria about the new housemaid. The girl had been engaged that morning, taking the place of one Anastasia Holmquist, a Black girl, who had sent a message by this girl, Julietta Aagaard, that she was leaving service of Fru Hansen, and had obtained Julietta to take her place.

"She seems a very quiet, good girl," added Honoria, "and she knows her duties."

"She is not of our village, eh?" enquired Cornelis, tentatively.

"No. She says she lives with her mother, somewhere up in the hills." Honoria indicated with a gesture the section of the island behind Fairfield.

Cornelis found his mind relieved. The girl was not of his village. Only one thing remained to be explained. He understood now why he had not observed the girl about the estate. But what had she been doing "bathing in the sea" at night? Such a practise was unheard of among the negroes. Few, indeed, would venture abroad or even out of their houses, unless necessity compelled, after dark. The houses themselves were closed up lightly, at nightfall, the doors of the cabins marked with crosses to keep out Jumbee—ghosts; their corrugated-iron roofs strewed with handfuls of sea-sand, the counting of which delayed the werewolf marauding nightly. A vast superstition ruled the lives of the Santa Crucian negroes with chains of iron. They believed in necromancy, witchcraft; they practised the obeah for sickness among themselves, took their vengeances with the aid of the Vauxdoux; practises brought in through Cartagena and Jamaica; from Dakar to the Congo mouths in the slave days; Obayi from Ashantee; Vauxdoux, worship of the Snake with its attendant horrors, through the savage Dahomeyans who had slaved for King Christophe in the sugar fields of Black Haiti.

To go from up in the hills to the sea, at night, for a bath—it was simply unheard of. Yet, the girl, seeing him there on the gallery, had been plainly startled. She had come from the sea. Her lithe body, the towel about her head, had been sea-damp that night. It was unheard of, unless—. Cornelis had learned something in the six months of his residence on Santa Cruz.

"Who is Julietta's mother?" he enquired suddenly.

Honoria did not know anything about Julietta's mother. This was the West End of Santa Cruz, and Honoria had lived all her life near Christiansted.

But, three days later, from a brow-beaten Alonzo, Cornelis learned the truth. The deference with which the young Julietta had been treated by the other servants, the Black People of his village, had been marked. Reluctantly Alonzo told his master the truth. Julietta's mother was the *mamaloi,* the witch-woman, of this portion of the island.Beyond satisfying his curiosity, this news meant little to Cornelis. He was too much a product of civilization, too much Caucasian, for the possible inferences to have their full effect upon him. It was not until some days later, when he surprized the look of sullen hatred in Julietta's swiftly drooped eyes, that it recurred to him; that the thought crossed his mind that Julietta had come into service in Fairfield House to retaliate upon him for her rejection. Hell hath no fury like a woman scorned! There was no Danish equivalent to the English proverb, or if there was, it lay outside Cornelis' knowledge. Yet, although a European Dane—despite the fact that his residence on Santa Cruz had not been long enough for him to realize what such deadly dislike as he had surprized in Julietta's glance might mean—Cornelis, no imbecile, did realize at the least a certain sense of discomfort.

Honoria, born on the island, could have helped the situation. But— there was no developed "situation." Cornelis wished this girl at the bottom of the sea; transplanted to another and distant island of the archipelago, but beyond that there was no more than the sense of discomfort at the girl's quiet, efficient presence about her duties in his house. He could not, of course, explain to his young wife his reasons for wishing lithe Julietta away.

thin linen flamed up, and with her stick she manipulated it until every particle of it was consumed, and then stirred the embers. A few sparks came out. The shirt was completely burned.

Her face drawn, she returned to the bedroom above. Cornelis was asleep. She sat beside his bed for two hours; then, after a long look at his flushed face, she departed silently for her own room.

In the morning the fever was broken. Many of the smaller pustules had disappeared. The remaining rash was going down. Cornelis, at her beseeching, remained in bed. At noon he arose. He felt perfectly well, he said.

"All that vexation about a little prickly heat!" Honoria sighed. She had four brothers. Men! They were much alike. How often had she heard her mother, and other mature women, say that!

That night Cornelis' skin was entirely restored. It was as though there had been no interval of burning agony. Cornelis, apparently, had forgotten that painful interval. But the reaction had made him especially cheerful at dinnertime. He laughed and joked rather more than usual. He did not even notice Julietta as she waited, silently, on the table.

Two nights later, at the dinner-table, Cornelis collapsed forward in the middle of a phrase. His face went deathly white, his lips suddenly dry, a searing pain like the thrust of a carving-knife through and through his chest. Sudden froth stood at the corners of his mouth. The table-edge athwart him alone kept him from falling prone. He hung there, in intolerable agony, for seconds. Then, slowly, as it had "gone in," the white-hot "knife" was withdrawn. He drew in a labored breath, and Honoria supported him upright. She had flown to him around the table.

As she stood upright propping him back into his chair, she saw Julietta. The brown girl's lips were drawn back from her even, beautiful teeth, her wide mouth in an animal-like snarl, her amber eyes boring into Cornelis' face, a very Greek-mask of hatred. An instant afterward, Julietta's face was that of the blank, submissive housemaid. But Honoria had seen.

At a bound her hands were clenched tight about the girl's slender arms and Julietta was being shaken like a willow wand in a great gale. Her tray, with glasses, shot resoundingly to the stone floor, to a tinkle of smashed glass. The Fighting Macartney blood showed red in Honoria's pallid face.

"It's you, then, you deadly creature, is it, eh? You who have done this devilish thing to your master! You—in my house! It was you, then, who made the rash, with your double-damned 'magic'!"

In the primitive urge of her fury at one who had struck at her man, Honoria had the slim brown girl against the room's wall now, holding her helpless in a grasp like steel with her own slender arms.

Cornelis, faint after that surge of unbearable, deadly pain, struggled to speak, there in his chair. Well-nigh helpless, he looked on at this unaccountable struggle. At last he found his voice, a voice faint and weak.

"What is it?—what is it, Honoria, my dear?"

"It's this witch!" cried Honoria through clenched teeth. "It is she who has put the *obeah* on you." Then, "You she-devil, you will take it off or I'll kill you here and now. Take it off, then! take it off!"Honoria's voice had risen to a menacing scream. The girl cowered, wiltingly, under her fierce attack.

"Ooh Gahd—me mistress! Ooh, Gahd! 'Taint I, ma'am, I swear to Gahd—I ain't do it, ma'am. Ooh, Gahd—me boans! Yo' break me, mistress. Fo' Gahd-love leave me to go!"

But Honoria, unrelaxed, the fighting-blood of her clan aroused, held the brown girl relentlessly.

"Take it off!" came, ever and again, through her small, clenched teeth. The brown girl began to struggle, ineffectually, gave it up, submitted to be held against the wall, her eyes now wide, frightened at this unexpected, sudden violence.

"What is it that you tell her to do?" This from Cornelis, recovering, shocked, puzzled.

"It is their damnable 'obi'," hissed Honoria. "I will make her 'take it off' you or I'll kill her."

'It is her mother," said Cornelis, suddenly inspired."I know about her mother. I asked. Her mother, this girl's mother, there in the hills—it is the girl's mother who does this wickedness."

Honoria suddenly shifted her desperate grip upon the girl's numb arms. She twisted, and Julietta's slender body, yielding, collapsed limply to the floor. With a lightning-like motion, back and then forward again, Honoria menaced her with the great carving-knife, snatched from before her husband.

"Get up!" Her voice was low now, deadly. "Get up, you devil, and lead me to your mother's house."

Julietta, trembling, silent, dragged herself to her feet. Honoria pointed to the door with the knife's great shining blade. In silence the girl slipped out, Honoria following. Cornelis sat, still numb with that fearful reaction after his unbearable pain, slumped forward now in his mahogany armchair at the head of his table. His bones felt like water. His head sank forward on his arms He remained motionless until Alonzo, the groom, summoned from the village by the frightened, gray-faced cook who had overheard, roused him, supported him upstairs.

The two women passed around the corner of Fairfield House, skirted the huddled cabins of the estate-village in silence, began to mount the steep hill at the back. Through tangled brush and twining, resistant guinea-grass, a slender trail wound abruptly upward into the deeper hills beyond. Up, and always up they went, the Caucasian lady grim and silent, the great knife held menacingly behind the unseeing back of the brown girl who stepped around turns and avoided roots and small rocks with the ease of custom.

At the head of the second ravine Honoria's conductress turned sharply to the right and led the way along the hill's edge toward a small clearing among the mahogany and tibet tree scrub. A dingy cabin, of wood, with the inevitable corrugated iron roof, hung perilously on the hill's seaward edge. Straight to its door walked Julietta, paused, tapped, opened the door, and pressed close by Honoria, entered.

A dark brown woman peered at them across a small table. With her thumb, Honoria noted, she was rubbing very carefully the side of a small waxllke thing, which glistened dully in the illumination of a small, smoky oil lamp standing on the table. The woman, her eyes glassy as though from the effects of some narcotic drug, peered dully at the intruders.

Honoria, her left hand clenched lightly on Julietta's wincing shoulder, confronted her, the knife's point resting on the table beside the brown hand which held the wax. This was molded, Honoria observed, to the rough simulacrum of a human being.

"That is my husband!" announced Honoria without preamble. "You will take your 'obi' off now. Otherwise I will kill you both!"

A long blackened needle lay beside the brown woman's hand on the table. She looked up into Honoria's face, dully.

"Yes, me mistress," she acquiesced in a singsong voice.

"You will do that at once!" Honoria tapped her knife-blade on the table decisively. "I am Fru Hansen. I was Honoria Macartney. I mean what I say. Come!"

The brown woman laid the wax image carefully down on table. She rose, dreamily, fumbled about in the semi-darkness of the cabin. She returned carrying a shining, new tin, half filled with water. This, as carefully as she had handled the wax image, she set down beside it. Then, as gingerly, she picked up the image, muttered a string of unintelligible words in the old Crucian Creole, thickly interspersed with Dahomeyan. Honoria recognized several of the words—"*caffoon,*" "*Shandramadan*"—but the sequence she could not grasp. The brown woman ended her speech, plunged the image into the water. She washed it carefully, as though it had been an incredibly tiny infant and she fearful of doing it some injury by clumsy handling. She removed it from the tin of water, the drops running down its surface of oily wax. She handed the image, with a suggestion of relaxed care now, to Honoria.

"Him aff, now, me mistress; I swear-yo', him aff! I swear yo' be Gahd, an' help me de Jesus!"

Honoria took the image into her hand, looked at it curiously in that dim light, made upon it with her thumb the sign of the cross. Then she slowly broke it into pieces, the sweat standing in beads on her face. She turned, without another word, and walked out of the cabin. As she proceeded down the trail, laboriously now, her legs weak in her high-heeled slippers, she cast crumbling bits of the wax right and left into the dense scrub among the bushes at the trail's sides. Her mouth and throat felt strangely dry. She murmured inarticulate prayers.

She limped into Fairfield House half an hour later and found Cornelis entirely restored. He asked her many questions, and to these she returned somewhat evasive answers. Yes—she had gone to Julietta's mother's cabin up the hill. Yes—the "stupidness" of these people needed a life-time to realize. No-there had been no difficulty. Julietta's mother was a "stupid" old creature. There would be no more trouble, she was sure. It was extraordinary what effects they could produce. They brought it with them from Africa, of course—stupidness, wickedness—and handed it down from generation to generation. . . .

She might have her own thoughts—men were very much alike, as her mother had said—as the days wore into weeks, the weeks to the placid years which lay before her, with her man, here at Fairfield for a while, later, perhaps, in some larger house, in a more important position.

What had caused that devilish little Julietta to contrive such a thing? Those eyes! that mouth! Honoria had seen the hatred in her face.

She would, of course, never ask Cornelis. Best to leave such matters alone. Men! She had fought for this man—her man.

She would give him of her full devotion. There would be children in time. She would have, to replace Julietta, a new housemaid. There was one she remembered, near Christiansted. She would drive over tomor-row. The affairs of a Santa Crucian wife!

Cornelis plainly loved her. He was hers. There would be deviled landcrabs, sprinkled with port wine, dusted with herbs; baked in the stone oven for breakfast. . . .

MRS. LORRIQUER

THE late Ronald Firbank, British author, apostle of the light touch in literary treatment, put grass skirts upon the three lady heroines of his West Indian Book, *Prancing Nigger,* as all persons who have perused that delicate romance of an unnamed West Indian island will doubtless remember. In so dressing Mrs. Mouth, and her two attractive daughters, Mr. Firbank was only twelve thousand miles out of the way, although that is not bad for anybody who writes about the West Indies—almost conservative, in fact. I, Gerald Canevin, have more than once reassured timid female inquirers, who had heard of our climate, but who were apprehensive of living among "those savages and cannibals!"I have always suspected that Mr. Firbank to go back for a moment to that gentleman before dismissing him and his book, got his light-touch information about the West Indies from a winter tour aboard one of the great trans-Atlantic liners which, winters, are used for such purposes in the Mediterranean and Caribbean, and which, in St. Thomas, discharge their hundreds of "personally conducted" tourists in swarms upon our innocent, narrow sidewalks, transforming the quiet, Old World town into a seething, hectic market-place for several hours every two weeks or so during a winter's season there.

For, truth being stranger by far than any fiction, there are grass skirts—on such occasions—on St. Thomas' streets; piles and stacks of them, for sale to tourists who buy them avidly. I know of no more engaging sight in this world than a two hundred and fifty pound tourist-lady, her husband in the offing, his hand in his money-pocket, chaffering with one of our Cha-Cha women with her drab, flat face and tight-pulled, straight hair knotted at the back, for a grass skirt!

It appears that, some years back, a certain iron-visaged spinster, in the employ of a social service agency, "took up" the Cha-Cha women, seeking to brighten their lot, and, realizing that a certain native raffia grass had commercial possibilities, taught them to make Polynesian grass skirts of it. Thereafter and ever since there has been a vast plague of these things about the streets of St. Thomas whenever a tourist vessel comes into our harbor under the skilled pilotage of Captain Simmons or Captain Caroc, our pilots.

I open this strange tale of Mrs. Lorriquer in this offhand fashion because my first sight of that compact, gray-haired little American gentlewoman was when I passed her, in the very heart and midst of one of these tourist invasions, rather indignantly trying to get rid of an insistent vender who seemed possessed to drape her five feet two, and one hundred and sixty pounds, in a five-colored grass skirt, and who would not be appeased and desist. As I was about to pass I overheard Mrs. Lorriquer say, with both indignation and finality:

"But, I'm not a tourist—I live here!"

That effectually settled the grass-skirt seller, who turned her attention to the tourists forthwith.

I had paused, almost unconsciously, and found myself face to face with Mrs. Lorriquer, whom I had not seen before. She smiled at me and I smiled back.

"Will you allow another permanent resident to rescue you from this mêlée?" I inquired, removing my hat.

"It is rather like a Continental *mardi gras,* isn't it?" said Mrs. Lorriquer, taking my arm."Where are you staying?" I inquired. "Are you at the Grand Hotel?"

"No," said Mrs. Lorriquer. "We have a house, the Crique place, half-way up Denmark Hill. We came down the day before yesterday, on the Nova Scotia, and we expect to be here all winter."

"I am Gerald Canevin," said I, "and I happen to be your very near neighbor. Probably we shall see a good deal of each other. If I can be of any assistance—"

"You have, already, Mr. Canevin," said Mrs. Lorriquer, whimsically.

I supposed at once she referred to my "rescue" of her from the tourist mob, but, it seemed, she had something quite different in her mind.

"It was because of some things of yours we had read," she went on, "that Colonel Lorriquer and I—and my widowed daughter, Mrs. Preston—decided to spend the winter here," she finished.

"Indeed!" said I. "Then, perhaps, you will allow me to continue the responsibility. When would it meet your convenience for me to call and meet the Colonel and Mrs. Preston?"

"Come any time," said Mrs. Lorriquer, "come to dinner, of course. We are living very informally."

We had reached the post-office, opposite the Grand Hotel, and here, doubtless according to instructions, stood Mrs. Lorriquer's car. I handed her in, and the kindly-faced, short, stout, little sixty-year-old lady was whirled away around the corner of the hotel toward one of the side roads which mount the precipitous sides of St. Thomas' best residential district.

I called the following afternoon, and thus inaugurated what proved to be a very pleasant acquaintanceship.

Colonel Lorriquer, a retired army engineer, was a man of seventy, extraordinarily well preserved, genial, a ripened citizen of the world. He had, it transpired on acquaintance, had a hand in many pieces of engineering, in various parts of the known world, and had spent several years on that vast American enterprise, the construction of the Panama Canal. Mrs. Preston, whose aviator husband had met his death a few months previously in the exercise of his hazardous profession, turned out to be a very charming person, still stunned and over-burdened with the grief of her bereavement, and with two tiny children. I gathered that it was largely upon her account that the Colonel and Mrs. Lorriquer had come to St. Thomas that winter. Being a West Indian enthusiast, it seemed to me that the family had used excellent judgment. There could be no better place for them under those circumstances. There is that in the charm and perfect climate of the Northern Lesser Antilles which heals the wounds of the heart, even though, as they say, when one stays too long there is Lethe.

We settled down in short order to a more or less intimate acquaintanceship. The Lorriquers, and Mrs. Preston, were, so to speak, "my sort of people." Many mutual acquaintances developed as we became better acquainted. We found much in common.

I have set down all this preliminary portion of this story thus in detail, because I have wished to emphasize, if possible, the fact that never, in all my experiences with the bizarre which this human scene offers to the open-minded observer, has it occurred to me to find any greater contrast than that which existed between Mrs. Lorriquer, short, stout, matter-of-fact, kindly little lady that she was, and the quite utterly incredible thing which—but I must not, I simply must not, in this case, allow myself to get ahead of my story. God knows it is strange enough not to need any "literary devices" to make it seem stranger.

The Lorriquers spent a good deal of the time which, under the circumstances, hung upon their hands, in card-playing. All three members of the family were expert Auction and Contract players. Naturally, being quite close at hand, I became a fourth and many evenings not otherwise occupied were spent, sometimes at my house, sometimes at theirs, about the card-table.

The Colonel and I played together, against the two ladies, and this arrangement was very rarely varied. Occasionally Mrs. Squire, a middle-aged woman who had known the Lorriquers at home in the States, and who had an apartment at the Grand Hotel for the winter, joined us, and then, usually, Mrs. Preston gave up her place and Mrs. Squire and I paired against the Colonel and his wife.

Even after the lapse of several years, I confess that I find myself as I write, hesitant, reluctant somehow, to set down the beginning of the strange discrepancy which first indicated what was to come to light in our innocent social relationship that winter. I think I can best do so, best open up this incredible thing, by recording a conversation between me and Mrs. Squire as we walked, one moonlit midnight, slowly down the hill toward the Grand Hotel.

We had finished an evening at the Lorriquers, and Mrs. Lorriquer had been especially, a little more than ordinarily, rude over the cards. Somehow, I can not say how it occurred, we discussed this strange anomaly in our hostess, usually the most kindly, simple, hospitable soul imaginable.

"She only does it when she plays cards," remarked Mrs. Squire. "Otherwise, as you have said, Mr. Canevin, she is the very soul of kindliness, of generosity. I have never been able to understand, and I have known the Lorriquers for more than ten years—how a woman of her character and knowledge of the world can act as she does over the card-table. It would be quite unbearable, quite utterly absurd—would it not—if one didn't know how very sweet and dear she really is."

It was, truly, a puzzle. It had developed very soon after we had started in at our Bridge games together. The plain fact, to set it down straight, was that Mrs. Lorriquer, *at the card-table,* was a most pernicious old termagant! A more complete diversity between her as she sat, frowning over her cards; exacting every last penalty; enforcing abstruse rules against her opponents while taking advantage of breaking them all herself *ad libitum;* arguing, most inanely and even offensively, over scores and value of points and penalties—all her actions and conduct at the card-table; with her general placidity, kindliness, and effusive good-nature under all other circumstances—a more complete diversity, I say, could never be imagined.It has always been one of my negative principles that annoyance over the details or over the outcome of any game of chance or skill should never be expressed. That sort of thing has always seemed to me absurd; indeed, inexcusable. Yet, I testify, I have, and increasingly as our acquaintance progressed, been so worked up over the cards when playing with the Lorriquer family, as to have to put the brakes down tight upon some expression of annoyance which I should later have regretted. Indeed, I will go farther, and own up to the fact that I have been badgered into entering into arguments with Mrs. Lorriquer at the table, when she would make some utterly outrageous claim, and then argue—the only word for it is *offensively*—against the massed testimony of her opponents and her partner for the evening. More than once, Mrs. Preston, under the stress of such an exhibition of temper and unreasonableness on her mother's part, has risen from the table, making some excuse, only to return a few minutes later. I believe that on all such occasions, Mrs. Preston took this means of allowing her annoyance to evaporate rather than express herself to her mother in the presence of a guest. To say that it was annoyance is to put it very mildly indeed. It was embarrassing, too, to the very last degree. The subjects upon which Mrs. Lorriquer would "go up in the air," as Mrs. Squire once modernly expressed it, were always trivial; always unreasonable. Mrs. Lorriquer, although a finished player in all respects, was, I think, always, as a matter of fact, in the wrong. She would question the amount of a score, for example, and, upon being shown the printed penalties for such score on the cover-page of the score pad, or from one of the standard books on the game, would shift over to a questioning of the score itself. The tricks, left on the table, would be counted out to her, before her eyes, by Colonel Lorriquer. Half-way through such an ocular demonstration, Mrs. Lorriquer would interrupt her husband with some kind of diatribe, worthy the mind of a person quite utterly ignorant of the game of Contract and of decent manners. She insisted upon keeping all scores herself, but unless this process were very carefully watched and checked, she would, perhaps half the time, cheat in favor of her own side.

It was, really, outrageous. Time and time again, I have gone home from the Lorriquers, after such an evening as I have indicated, utterly resolved never to play there again, or to refuse, as courteously as might be possible, to meet Mrs. Lorriquer over a card-table. Then, the next day, perhaps, the other Mrs. Lorriquer, charming, kindly, sweet-natured, gentle and hospitable, would be in such overwhelming, disarming evidence, that my overnight resolution would be dissipated into thin air, and I would accuse myself of becoming middle-aged, querulous!

But this unaccountable diversity between the Mrs. Lorriquer of ordinary affairs and the Mrs. Lorriquer of the card-table, outstanding, conspicuous, absurd indeed, as it was, was really as nothing when compared to Mrs. Lorriquer's luck at the cards.

I have never seen anything like it; never heard, save in old-fashioned fictional tales of the person who sold his soul to Satan for invincibility at cards, of anything which could compare to it. It is true that Mrs. Lorriquer sometimes lost—a single game, or perhaps even a rubber. But, in the long run, Mrs. Lorriquer, even on the lowest possible basis for expressing what I mean, did not need to cheat, still less to argue over points or scores. She won, steadily, inevitably, monotonously, like the steady propulsive motions of some soulless machine at its mechanical work. It was virtually impossible to beat her.

We did not play for stakes. If we had, a goodly portion of my income would have diverted that winter to the Lorriquer coffers. Save for the fact that as it was the Colonel who played partners with me, it would have been Mrs. Lorriquer, rather than the Lorriquer family, who would have netted all the proceeds!

In bidding, and, indeed, in the actual playing of a hand, she seemed to follow no system beyond abject reliance on her "luck." I have, not once, but many, many times, known her, for example, to bid two no-trump originally, on a hand perhaps containing two "singletons," only to have her partner "go to three" with a hand containing every card which she needed for the dummy. I will not specify, beyond this, any technical illustrations of how her extraordinary luck" manifested itself. Suffice it to say that Bridge is, largely, a mathematical matter, varied, in the case of four thoroughly trained players, by what is known as the "distribution" of the cards. It is this unknown element of "distribution" which keeps the game, in the hands of a table of experts, a "game of chance" and not merely a mathematical certainty gaged by skilful, back-and-forth, informative bidding. To put the whole matter of Mrs. Lorriquer's "luck" into a nutshell, it was this element of "distribution" of the cards which favored her, in and out of season; caused her to win with a continuous regularity; never seeming to cause her to be pleased at her success and so lend to an evening at cards with her at the table that rather unsatisfactory geniality which even a child shows when it "gets the breaks" at a game.

No; Mrs. Lorriquer was, while engaged in playing Bridge, a harridan, a disagreeable old vixen; a "pill" as, I believe, I once heard the outraged Mrs. Squire mutter desperately, under her breath!

Perhaps it would be an exaggeration to allege that as against the Colonel and me, playing as partners for many evenings, the "distribution" of the cards was adverse with absolute uniformity. I should hesitate to say that, positively, although my recollection is that such was the case. But, in the ordinary run of affairs, once in a while one of us would get a commanding hand, and, immune from the possibility of the "distribution" affecting success, would play it out to a winning score for the time being. It was after one such hand—I played it, the Colonel's hand as dummy—that I succeeded in making my bid: four hearts, to a game. I remember that I had nine hearts in my hand, together with the ace, king of clubs, and the "stoppers" on one other suit, and finishing with something "above the line" besides "making game" in one hand, that my first intimation of a strange element in Mrs. Lorriquer's attitude to the game made itself apparent. Hitherto—it was, perhaps, a matter of a month or six weeks of the acquaintance between us—it had been a combination of luck and what I can only call bad manners; the variety of luck which I have attempted to indicate and the "bad manners" strictly limited to such times as we sat around the square table in the center of the Lorriquers' breezy hall.

The indication to which I have referred was merely an exclamation from my right, where Mrs. Lorriquer sat, as usual, in her accustomed place.

"Sapristi!" boomed Mrs. Lorriquer, in a deep, resonant, man-like voice. I looked up from my successful hand and smiled at her. I had, of course, imagined that she was joking—to use an antique, rather meaningless, old-French oath, in that voice. Her own voice, even when scolding over the card-table, was a light, essentially feminine voice. If she had been a singer, she would have been a thin, high soprano.

To my surprize, Mrs. Lorriquer was not wearing her whimsical expression. At once, too, she entered into an acrimonious dispute with the Colonel over the scoring of our game-going hand, as usual, insisting on something quite ridiculous, the old Colonel arguing with her patiently.

I glanced at Mrs. Preston to see what she might have made of her mother's exclamation in that strange, unaccustomed, incongruous voice. She was looking down at the table, on which her hands rested, a pensive and somewhat puzzled expression puckering her white forehead. So far as I could guess from her expression, she too, had been surprised at what she had heard. Apparently, I imagined, such a peculiar manifestation of annoyance on Mrs. Lorriquer's part was as new to her daughter as it was to me, still a comparative stranger in that family's acquaintance.

We resumed play, and, perhaps an hour or more later, it happened that we won another rather notable hand, a little slam, carefully bid up, in no-trump, the Colonel playing the hand. About half-way through, when it was apparent that we were practically sure of our six over-tricks, I noticed, being, of course, unoccupied, that Mrs. Lorriquer, at my right, was muttering to herself, in a peculiarly ill-natured, querulous way she had under such circumstances, and, my mind stimulated by the remembrance of her use of the old-French oath, I listened very carefully and discovered that she was muttering in French. The most of it I lost, but the gist of it was, directed toward her husband, a running diatribe of the most personal and even venomous kind imaginable.

Spanish, as I was aware, Mrs. Lorriquer knew. She had lived in the Canal Zone for a number of years, and elsewhere where the Colonel's professional engagements as an engineer had taken them, but, to my knowledge, my hostess was unacquainted with colloquial French. The mutterings were distinctively colloquial. She had, among other things, called her husband in those mutterings "the accursed child of a misbegotten frog," which is, however inelegant on the lips of a cultivated elderly gentlewoman, at least indicative of an intimate knowledge of the language of the Prankish peoples! No one else sensed it—the foreign tongue, I mean—doubtless because both other players were fully occupied, the Colonel in making our little slam, Mrs. Preston in doing what she could to prevent him, and besides, such mutterings were common on Mrs. Lorriquer's part; were usual, indeed, on rare occasions when a hand at Bridge was going against her and her partner. It was the use of the French that intrigued me.

A few days later, meeting her coming down the hill, a sunny smile on her kindly, good-humored face, I addressed her, whimsically, in French. Smilingly, she disclaimed all knowledge of what I was talking about.

"I supposed you were a French scholar, somehow," said I.

"I really don't know a word of it," replied Mrs. Lorriquer, "unless, perhaps, what 'R. S. V. P.' means, and—oh, yes!—'honi soit qui mal y pense!' That's on the great seal of England, isn't it, Mr. Canevin?" It set me to wondering, as, I imagine, it would have set anyone under just those circumstances, and I had something to puzzle over. I could not, you see, readily reconcile Mrs. Lorriquer's direct statement that she knew no French, a statement made with the utmost frankness, and to no possible end if it were untrue, with the fact that she had objurgated the Colonel under her breath and with a surprizing degree of fluency, as "the accursed child of a misbegotten frog!"

It seemed, this little puzzle, insoluble! There could, it seemed to me, be no possible question as to Mrs. Lorriquer's veracity. If she said she knew no French besides the trite phrases which everybody knows, then the conclusion was inevitable; she knew no French! But—beyond question she had spoken, under her breath to be sure, but in my plain hearing, in that language and in the most familiar and colloquial manner imaginable.

There was, logically, only one possible explanation. Mrs. Lorriquer had been speaking French without her own knowledge! I had to let it go at that, absurd as such a conclusion seemed to me.

But, pondering over this apparent absurdity, another point, which might have been illuminating if foresight were as satisfactory as "hindsight," emerged in my mind. I recalled that what I have called "the other Mrs. Lorriquer" was an especially gentle, kindly person, greatly averse to the spoiling of anybody's good time! The normal Mrs. Lorriquer was, really, almost softly apologetic. The least little matter wherein anything which could possibly be attributed to her had gone wrong would always be the subject of an explanation, an apology. If the palm salad at one of her luncheons or dinner did not seem to her to be quite perfect, there would be deprecatory remarks. If the limes from which a little juice was to be squeezed out upon the halved papayas at her table happened not to be of the highest quality, the very greenest of green limes that is, Mrs. Lorriquer would lament the absence of absolutely perfect limes that morning when she had gone in person to procure them from the market-place. In other words, Mrs. Lorriquer carried almost to the last extreme her veritable passion for making her guests enjoy themselves, for seeing to it that everybody about her was happy and comfortable and provided with the best of everything.

But—it occurred to me that she never apologized afterward for any of her exhibitions at the card-table.

By an easy analogy, the conclusion—if correct—was inevitable. Mrs. Lorriquer, apparently, did not at all realize that she was a virtually different person when she played cards.

I pondered this, too. I came to the conclusion that, queer as it seemed, this was the correct explanation of her extraordinary conduct.

But—such an "explanation" did not carry one very far, that was certain. For at once it occurred to me as it would have occurred to anybody else, her husband and daughter for choice, that there must he something behind this "explanation." If Mrs. Lorriquer "was not herself" at such times as she was engaged in playing cards, what made her that way? I recalled, whimsically, the remark of a small child of my acquaintance whose mother had been suffering from a devastating sick-headache. Lillian's father had remarked:

"Don't trouble Mother, my dear. Mother's not herself this afternoon, you see."

"Well," countered the puzzled Lillian, "who is she, then, Daddy?"

It was, indeed, in this present case, quite as though Mrs. Lorriquer were somebody else, somebody quite different from "herself" whenever she sat at the card-table. That was as far as I could get with my attempt at any "explanation."

The "somebody else," as I thought the matter through, had three known characteristics. First, an incredibly ugly disposition. Second, the ability to speak fluently a language unknown to Mrs. Lorriquer. Third, at least as manifested on one occasion, and evidenced by no more than the booming utterance of a single word, a deep, man-like, bass voice!

I stopped there in my process of reasoning. The whole thing was too absurdly bizarre for me to waste any more time over it along that line of reasoning. As to the obvious process of consulting Colonel Lorriquer or Mrs. Preston, their daughter, on such a subject, that was, sheerly, out of the question. Interesting as the problem was to me, one simply does not do such things.

Then, quite without any warning, there came another piece of evidence. I have mentioned our St. Thomas Cha- Chas, and also that Mrs.

Lorriquer was accustomed to visit the market-place in person in the interest of her table. The St. Thomas Cha-Chas form a self-sustaining, self-contained community as distinct from the rest of the life which surrounds them in their own "village" set on the seashore to the west of the main portion of the town as oil from water. They have been there from time immemorial, the local "poor whites," hardy fishermen, faithful workers, the women great sellers of small hand-made articles (like the famous grass skirts) and garden produce. They are inbred, from a long living in a very small community of their own, look mostly all alike, and, coming as they did many years ago from the French island of St. Bartholomew, most of them when together speak a kind of modified Norman French, a peasant dialect of their own, although all of them know and use a simplified variety of our English tongue for general purposes.

Along the streets, as well as in the public market-place, the Cha-Cha women may be seen, always separate from the negress market-vendors, offering their needlework, their woven grass baskets and similar articles, and the varying seasonal fruits and vegetables which they cultivate in their tiny garden patches or gather from the more inaccessible distant groves and ravines of the island—mangoes, palmets, sugar-apples, the strange-appearing cashew fruits, every variety of local eatable including trays of the most villainous-appearing peppermint candy, which, upon trial, is a truly delicious confection.

Passing the market one morning I saw Mrs. Lorriquer standing in a group of five or six Cha-Cha market women who were outvying one another in presenting the respective claims of various trays loaded with the small, red, round tomatoes in which certain Cha-Cha families specialize. One of the women, in her eagerness to attract the attention of the customer, jostled another, who retaliated upon her in her own familiar tongue. An argument among the women broke out at this, several taking sides, and in an instant Mrs. Lorriquer was the center of a tornado of vocables in Cha-Cha French.

Fearing that this would be annoying to her, I hastened across the street to the market-place, toward the group, but my interference proved not to be required. I was, perhaps, half-way across when Mrs. Lorriquer took charge of the situation herself and with an effectiveness which no one could have anticipated. In that same booming voice with which she had ejaculated *"Sapristi!"* and in fluent, positively *Apache* French, Mrs. Lorriquer suddenly put a benumbing silence upon the bickering market women, who fell back from her in an astounded silence, so sudden a silence that clear and shrill came the comment from a near-by Black woman balancing a tray loaded to the brim with avocado pears upon her kerchiefed head, listening, pop-eyed, to the altercation. "Ooh, me Gahd!" remarked the negress to the air about her. "Whoite missy tahlk to they in Cha-Cha!"

It was only a matter of seconds before I was at Mrs. Lorriquer's side.

"Can I be of any assistance?" I inquired.

Mrs. Lorriquer glared at me, looking precisely as she did when engaged in one of her querulous, acrimonious arguments at the card-table. Then her countenance changed with a startling abruptness, and she looked quite as usual.

"I was just buying some of these lovely little tomatoes," she said.

The Cha-Cha women, stultified, huddled into a cowering knot, looked at her speechlessly, their red faces several shades paler than their accustomed brick-color. The one whose tray Mrs. Lorriquer now approached shrank back from her. I do not wonder, after the blast which this gentle-looking little American lady had but now let loose upon them all. The market seemed unusually quiet. I glanced about. Every eye was upon us. Fortunately, the marketplace was almost empty of customers.

"I'll take two dozen of these," said Mrs. Lorriquer. "How much are they, please?"

The woman counted out the tomatoes with hands trembling, placed them carefully in a paper bag, handed them to Mrs. Lorriquer, who paid her. We stepped down to the ground from the elevated concrete floor of the market.

"They seem so subdued—the poor souls!" remarked Mrs. Lorriquer, whose goggle-eyed chauffeur, a boy as black as ebony, glanced at her out of the corner of a fearfully rolled eye as he opened the door of her car.

"Come to luncheon," said Mrs. Lorriquer, sweetly, beaming at me, "and help us eat these nice little tomatoes. They are delicious with mayonnaise after they are blanched and chilled." It seemed rather an abrupt contrast, these homely words of invitation, after what I had heard her call those Cha-Cha women.

"I'll come, with pleasure," I replied.

"One o'clock, then," said Mrs. Lorriquer, nodding and smiling, as her Black Hans turned the car skilfully and started along the Queen's Road toward the center of town.

We did not play cards that afternoon after luncheon, because Mrs. Lorriquer and Mrs. Preston were going to an afternoon party at the residence of the Government Secretary's wife, and Colonel Lorriquer and I sat, over our coffee, on the west gallery of the house out of reach of the blazing early-afternoon sun, and chatted.

We got upon the subject of the possibility of another isthmian canal, the one tentatively proposed across Nicaragua.

"That, as you know, Mr. Canevin, was one of the old French Company's proposals, before they settled down to approximately the present site—the one we followed out—back in the late Seventies."

"De Lesseps," I murmured.

"Yes," said the Colonel, musingly, "yes—a very complex matter it was, that French proposal. They never could, it seems, have gone through with it, as a matter of fact—the opposition at home in France, the under-estimate of the gross cost of excavation, the suspicion of 'crookedness' which arose—they impeached the Count de Lesseps finally, you know, degraded him, ruined the poor fellow. And then, the sanitation question, you know. If it had not been for our Gorgas and his marvelous work in that direction—"

"Tell me," I interrupted, "just how long were the French at work on their canal, Colonel?"

"Approximately from 1881 to 1889," replied the Colonel, "although the actual work of excavation, the bulk of the work, was between '85 and '89. By the way, Canevin, we lived in a rather unusual house there. Have I ever mentioned that to you?"

"Never," said I. "What was the unusual element about your house?"

"Only that it was believed to be haunted," replied the Colonel; "although, I must admit, I never—we never—met with the least evidence outside the superstitions of the people. Our neighbors all believed it to be haunted in some way. We got it for a song for that reason and it was a very pleasant place. You see, it had been fitted up, quite regardless of the cost, as a kind of public casino or gambling-house, about 1885, and it had been a resort for de Lesseps' crowd for the four years before the French Company abandoned their work. It was a huge place, with delightful galleries. The furniture, too, was excellent. We took it as it stood, you see, and, beyond a terrific job to get it clean and habitable, it was a very excellent investment. We were there for more than three years altogether."

An idea, vague, tenuous, grotesque enough in all truth, and, indeed, somewhat less than half formed, had leaped into my mind at the combination of a "haunted" residence and the French work on the ill-fated le Lesseps canal project.

"Indeed!" said I. "It certainly sounds interesting. And do you know, Colonel, who ran the old casino; who, so to speak, was the proprietor—unless it was a part of the Company's scheme for keeping their men interested?"

"It was privately managed," returned the Colonel, "and, queerly enough, as it happens, I can show you the photograph of the former proprietor. He was a picturesque villain!"

The Colonel rose and started to go inside the house from where we sat on the cool gallery. He paused at the wide doorway, his hand on the jamb.

"It was the proprietor who was supposed to haunt the house," said he, and went inside.

My mind reeled under the stress of these clues and the attempts, almost subconscious—for, indeed, I had thought much of the possible problem presented by Mrs. Lorriquer's case; a "case" only in my own imagination, so far; and I had constructed tentatively three or four connected theories by the time the Colonel returned, a large, stiff, cabinet photograph in his hand. He laid this on the table between us and resumed his Chinese rattan lounge-chair. I picked up the photograph.

It was the portrait, stiffly posed. the hand, senatorially, in the fold of the long, black *surtout* coat, of the sort anciently known as a Prince Albert, of a rather small, emaciated man, whose face was disfigured by the pittings of smallpox; a man with a heavy head of jet-black hair, carefully combed after a fashion named, in our United States, for General McClellan of Civil War fame, the locks brushed forward over the tops of the ears and the parting, although this could not be seen in the front-face photograph, extending all the way down the back to the neck. A "croupier's" moustache, curled and waxed ferociously, ornamented the sallow, sinister features of a face notable only for its one outstanding feature; a jaw as solid and square as that of Julius Caesar. Otherwise, as far as character was concerned, the photograph showed a very unattractive person, the type of man, quite obviously, who in these modern times would inevitably have followed one of our numerous and varied "rackets" and probably, one imagined, with that jaw to help, successfully!"And how, if one may ask," said I, laying the photograph down on the table again, "did you manage to get hold of this jewel, Colonel Lorriquer?"

The old gentleman laughed. "We found it in the back of a bureau drawer," said he. "I have mentioned that we took the house over just as it was. Did you notice the cameo?"

"Yes," I replied, picking the photograph up once more to look at the huge breast-pin which seemed too large in the picture even for the enormous "de Joinville" scarf which wholly obliterated the shirt-front underneath.

"It is certainly a whopper!" I commented. "It reminds me of that delightful moving picture *Cameo Kirby*, if you happened to see it some time ago, on the silent screen.""Quite," agreed Colonel Lorriquer. "That, too, turned up, and in the same ancient bureau, when we were cleaning it. It was wedged in behind the edge of the bottom-board of the middle drawer. Of course you have observed that Mrs. Lorriquer wears it?"

I had, and said so. The enormous breast-pin was the same which I had many times observed upon Mrs. Lorriquer. It seemed a favorite ornament of hers. I picked up the photograph once more.

Down in the lower right-hand corner, in now faded gilt letters of ornamental scrollwork, appeared, the name of the photographer. I read: "La Palma, Quezaltenango."

"Quezaltenango,' I read aloud. "That is in Guatemala. Was the 'Gentleman of the house,' perhaps, a Central American? It would be hard to guess at his nationality from this. He looks a citizen of the world!"

"No," replied the Colonel, "he was a Frenchman, and he had been, as it appears, living by his wits all over Central America. When the work of construction actually began under the French Company—that was in 1885—there was a rush of persons like him toward the pickings from so large a group of men who would be looking for amusement, and this fellow came early and stayed almost throughout the four years. His name was Simon Legrand, and, from what I gathered about him, he was a very ugly customer."

"You remarked that he was connected with the alleged haunting," I ventured. "Is there, perhaps, a story in that?"

"Hardly a story, Mr. Canevin. No. It was merely that toward the end of the French Company's activities, in 1889, Legrand, who had apparently antagonized all his patrons at his casino, got into a dispute with one of them, over a game of *piquet* or *écarté*—one of those French games of some kind, perhaps even *vingt-et-un,* for all I know, or even *chemin-de-fer*—and Simon went up to his bedroom, according to the story, to secure a pistol, being, for the time, rather carelessly in that company, unarmed. His 'guest' followed him upstairs and shot him as he stood in front of the bureau where he kept his weapon, from the bedroom doorway, thus ending the career of what must have been a very precious rascal. Thereafter, the French Company's affairs and that of the casino being abruptly dissolved at about the same time, the rumor arose that Legrand was haunting his old quarters. Beyond the rumor, there never seemed anything to suggest its basis in anything but the imagination of the native Panamanians. As I have mentioned, we lived in the house three years, and it was precisely like any other house, only rather cheap, which satisfied us very well!"That, as a few cautious questions, put diplomatically, clearly showed, was all the Colonel knew about Simon Legrand and his casino. I used up all the questions I had in mind, one after another, and, it being past three in the afternoon, and overtime for the day's siesta, I was about to take my leave in search of forty winks and the afternoon's shower-bath, when the Colonel volunteered a singular piece of information. He had been sitting rather quietly, as though brooding, and it was this, which I attributed to the after-luncheon drowsiness germane to these latitudes, which had prompted me to go. I was, indeed, rising from my chair at the moment, when the Colonel remarked:

"One element of the old casino seemed to remain—perhaps that was the haunting!" He stopped, and I hung, poised, as it were, to catch what he might be about to say. He paused, however, and I prompted him.

"And what might that be, sir?" I asked, very quietly. The Colonel seemed to come out of his revery.

"Eh?" he said, "eh, what?" He looked at me rather blankly.

"You were remarking that one element of the old casino's influence seemed to remain in your Canal Zone residence," said I.

"Ah—yes. Why, it was strange, Mr. Canevin, distinctly strange. I have often thought about it; although, of course, it was the merest coincidence. unless—perhaps—well, the idea of *suggestion* might come into play. Er—ah—er, what I had in mind was that—er—Mrs. Lorriquer you know—she began to take up card-playing there. She had never, to my knowledge, played before; had never cared for cards in the least; been brought up, in early life, to regard them as not quite the thing for a lady and all that, you see. Her mother, by the way, was Sarah Langhorne—perhaps you had not heard this, Mr. Canevin—the very well-known medium of Bellows Falls, Vermont. The old lady had quite a reputation in her day. Strictly honest, of course! Old New England stock—of the very best, sir. Straight-laced! Lord—a card in the house would have been impossible! Cards, in that family! 'The Devil's Bible,' Mr. Canevin. That was the moral atmosphere which surrounded my wife's formative days. But—no sooner had we begun to live in that house down there, than she developed 'card-sense,' somehow, and she has found it—er—her chief interest, I should say, ever since." The old Colonel heaved a kind of mild sigh, and that was as near as I had heard to any comment on his wife's outrageous conduct at cards, which must, of course, have been a major annoyance in the old gentleman's otherwise placid existence.I went home with much material to ponder. I had enough to work out a more or less complete "case" now, if, indeed, there was an occult background for Mrs. Lorriquer's diverse conduct, her apparently subconscious use of colloquial French, and—that amazing deep bass voice!

Yes, all the elements seemed to be present now. The haunted house, with that scar-faced croupier as the haunter; the sudden predilection for cards emanating there; the initial probability of Mrs. Lorriquer's susceptibility to discarnate influences, to a control," as the spiritualists name this phenomenon—the cameo—all the rest of it; it all pointed straight to one conclusion, which, to put it conservatively, might be described as the "influence" of the late Simon Legrand's personality upon kindly Mrs. Lorriquer who had "absorbed" it in three years' residence in a house thoroughly impregnated by his ugly and unpleasant personality.

I let it go at that, and—it must be understood—I was only half-way in earnest at the time, in even attempting to attribute to this "case" any thing like an occult background. One gets to look for such explanations when one lives in the West Indies where the very atmosphere is charged with Magic!

But—my inferences, and whereunto these led, were, at their most extreme, mild, compared with what was, within two days, to be revealed to us all. However, I have resolved to set this tale down in order, as it happened, and again I remind myself that I must not allow myself to run ahead of the normal sequence of events. The *denouement,* however. did not take very long to occur.It was, indeed, no more than two days later, at the unpropitious hour of two-fifteen in the morning—I looked at my watch on my bureau as I was throwing on a few necessary clothes—that I was aroused by a confused kind of tumult outside, and, coming into complete wakefulness, observed an ominous glow through my windows and realized that a house, quite near by, was on fire.

I leaped at once out of bed, and took a better look, with my head out the window. Yes, it was a fire, and, from appearances, the makings of a fine—and very dangerous—blaze here in the heart of the residence district where the houses, on the sharp side-hill, are built very close together.

It was a matter of moments before I was dressed, after a fashion, and outside, and running down the path to my gateway and thence around the corner to the left. The fire itself, as I now saw at a glance, was in a wooden building now used as a garage, directly on the roadway before one of the Denmark Hill's ancient and stately mansions. Already a thin crowd, of negroes, entirely, had gathered, and I saw that I was "elected" to take charge in the absence of any other white man, when I heard, with relief, the engine approaching. Our Fire Department, while not hampered with obsolete apparatus, is somewhat primitive. The engine rounded the corner, and just behind it, a Government Ford, the "transportation" apportioned to Lieutenant Farnum of Uncle Sam's efficient Marines. The Lieutenant, serving as the Governor's Legal Aide, had, among his fixed duties, the charge of the Fire Department. This highly efficient young gentleman, whom I knew very well, was at once in the very heart of the situation, had the crowd back away to a reasonable distance, the fire engine strategically placed, and a double stream of chemicals playing directly upon the blazing shack.

The fire, however, had had a long start, and the little building was in a full blaze. It seemed, just then, doubtful whether or not the two streams would prove adequate to put it out. The real danger, however, under the night trade wind, which was blowing lustily, was in the spread of the fire, through flying sparks, of which there were many, and I approached Lieutenant Farnum offering cooperation.

"I'd suggest waking up the people—in that house, and that, and that one," directed Lieutenant Farmun, denoting which houses he had in mind.

"Right!" said I, "I'm shoving right off!" And I started down the hill to the first of the houses. On the way I was fortunate enough to meet my house-boy, Stephen Penn, an intelligent young negro, and him I dispatched to two of the houses which stood together, to awaken the inmates if, indeed, the noise of the conflagration had not already performed that office. Then I hastened at a run to the Crique place, occupied by the Lorriquer family, the house farthest from the blaze, yet in the direct line of the sparks and blazing slivers which the trade wind carried in a thin aerial stream straight toward it.

Our servants, in West Indian communities, never remain for the night on the premises. The Lorriquers would be, like all other Caucasians, alone in their house. I had, as it happened, never been upstairs in the house; did not, therefore, have any idea of its layout, nor knew which of the bedrooms were occupied by the several members of the family.

Without stopping to knock at the front entrance door, I slipped the latch of a pair of jalousies leading into the "hall" or drawing-room, an easy matter to negotiate, stepped inside across the window-sill, and, switching on the electric light in the lower entranceway, ran up the broad stone staircase to the floor above. I hoped that chance would favor me in finding the Colonel's room first, but as there was no way of telling, I rapped on the first door I came to, and, turning the handle—this was an emergency--stepped inside, leaving the door open behind me to secure such light as came from the single bulb burning in the upper hallway.

I stepped inside.

Again, pausing for an instant to record my own sensations as an integral portion of this narrative, I hesitate, but this time only because of the choices which lie before me in telling, now long afterward, with the full knowledge of what was involved in this strange case, precisely what I saw; precisely what seemed to blast my eyesight for its very incredibleness—its "impossibility."

I had, it transpired, hit upon Mrs. Lorriquer's bedroom, and there plain before me—it was a light, clear night, and all the eight windows stood open to the starlight and what was left of a waning moon—lay Mrs. Lorriquer on the stub-posted mahogany four-poster with its tester and valance. The mosquito-net was not let down, and Mrs. Lorriquer, like most people in our climate, was covered, as she lay in her bed, only with a sheet. I could. therefore, see her quite plainly, in an excellent light.

But—that was not all that I saw.

For, beside the bed, quite close in fact, stood—Simon Legrand— facing me, the clothes, the closely buttoned *surtout,* the spreading, flaring *de Joinville* scarf, fastened with the amazing brooch, the pock-marked. ill-natured face, the thick, black hair, the typical*croupier* moustache, the truculent expression, Simon Legrand, to the last detail, precisely as he appeared in the cabinet photograph of La Palma of Quezaltenango—Simon Legrand to the life.And, between him as be stood there, glaring truculently at me, intruding upon his abominable manifestation, and the body of Mrs. Lorriquer, as I glared back at this incredible configuration, there stretched, and wavered, and seemed to flow, *toward* him and *from* the body of Mrs. Lorriquer, a whitish, tenuous stream of some milky-looking material—like a waved sheet, like a great mass of opaque soap-bubbles, like those pouring grains of attenuated *plasma* described in *Dracula;* when in the dreadful castle in Transylvania, John Harker stood confronted with the materialization of that arch-fiend's myrmidons.All these comparisons rushed through my mind, and, finally, the well-remembered descriptions of what takes plate in the "materialization" of a "control" at a mediumistic séance when material from the medium floats toward and into the growing incorporation of the manifestation, building up the nonfictitious body through which the control expresses itself.

All this, I say, rushed through my mind with the speed of thought, and recorded itself so that I can easily remember the sequence of these ideas. But, confronted with this utterly unexpected affair, what I did, in actuality, was to pause, transfixed with the strangeness, and to mutter, "My God!"

Then, shaking internally, pulling myself together by a mighty effort while the shade or manifestation or whatever it might prove to be, of the French gambler glowered at me murderously, in silence, I made a great effort, one of those efforts which a man makes under the stress of utter necessity. I addressed the figure—in French!

"Good-morning, Monsieur Legrand," said I, trying to keep the quaver out of my voice. "Is it too early, think you, for a little game of *ecarte?"* Just how, or why, this sentence formed itself in my mind, or, indeed, managed to get itself uttered, is to this day, a puzzle to me. It seemed just then the one appropriate, the inevitable way, to deal with the situation. Then—

In the same booming bass which had voiced Mrs. Lorriquer's *"Sapristi",* a voice startlingly in contrast with his rather diminutive figure, Simon Legrand replied: *"Oui, Monsieur,* at your service on all occasions, day or night—you to select the game!" *"Eh bien, donc—"* I began, when there came an interruption in the form of a determined masculine voice just behind me. "Put your hands straight up and keep them there!"

I turned, and looked straight into the mouth of Colonel Lorriquer's service revolver; behind it the old Colonel, his face stern, his steady grip on the pistol professional, uncompromising.

At once he lowered the weapon.

"What—Mr. Canevin!" he cried. "What—"

"Look!" I cried back at him, "look, while it lasts, Colonel!" and, grasping the old man's arm, I directed his attention to the now rapidly fading form or simulacrum of Simon Legrand. The Colonel stared fixedly at this amazing sight.

"My God!" He repeated my own exclamation. Then—"It's Legrand, Simon Legrand, the gambler!"

I explained, hastily, disjointedly, about the fire. I wanted the Colonel to understand, first, what I was doing in his house at half-past two in the morning. That, at the moment, seemed pressingly important to me. I had hardly begun upon this fragmentary explanation when Mrs. Preston appeared at the doorway of her mother's room.

"Why, it's Mr. Canevin!" she exclaimed. Then, proceeding, "There's a house on fire quite near by, Father—I thought I'd best awaken you and Mother." Then, seeing that, apart from my mumbling of explanations about the fire, both her father and I were standing, our eyes riveted to a point near her mother's bed, she fell silent, and not unnaturally, looked in the same direction. We heard her, behind us, her voice now infiltrated with a sudden alarm:

"What is it?—*what is it?* Oh, Father, I thought I saw—"The voice trailed out into a whisper. We turned, simultaneously, thus missing the very last thin waning appearance of Simon Legrand as the stream of tenuous, wavering substance poured back from him to the silent, immobile body of Mrs. Lorriquer motionless on its great bed, and the Colonel was just in time to support his daughter as she collapsed in a dead faint.

All this happened so rapidly that it is out of the question to set it down so as to give a mental picture of the swift sequence of events.

The Colonel, despite his character and firmness, was an old man, and not physically strong. I therefore lifted Mrs. Preston and carried her to a day-bed which stood along the wall of the room and there laid her down. The Colonel rubbed her hands. I fetched water from the mahogany washstand such as is part of the furnishing of all these old West Indian residence bedrooms, and sprinkled a little of the cool water on her face. Within a minute or two her eyelids fluttered, and she awakened. This secondary emergency had naturally diverted our attention from what was toward at Mrs. Lorriquer's bedside. But now, leaving Mrs. Preston who was nearly herself again, we hastened over to the bed.

Mrs. Lorriquer, apparently in a very deep sleep, and breathing heavily, lay there, inert. The Colonel shook her by the shoulder; shook her again. Her head moved to one side, her eyes opened, a baleful glare in her eyes.

"Va t'en, sâle bête!" said a deep man-like voice from between her clenched teeth. Then, a look of recognition replacing the glare, she sat up abruptly, and, in her natural voice, addressing the Colonel whom she had but now objurgated as a "foul beast," she asked anxiously:"Is anything the matter, dearest? Why—Mr. Canevin—I hope nothing's wrong!"

I told her about the fire.

In the meantime Mrs. Preston, somewhat shaky, but brave though puzzled over the strange happenings which she had witnessed, came to her mother's bedside. The Colonel placed an arm about his daughter, steadying her.

"Then we'd better all get dressed," said Mrs. Lorriquer, when I had finished my brief account of the fire, and the Colonel and I and Mrs. Preston walked out of the bedroom. Mrs. Preston slipped into her own room and closed the door behind her.

"Get yourself dressed, sir," I suggested to the old Colonel, "and I will wait for you on the front gallery below." He nodded, retired to his room, and I slipped downstairs and out to the gallery, where I sank into a cane chair and lit a cigarette with shaking fingers.

The Colonel joined me before the cigarette was smoked through. He went straight to the point.

"For God's sake, what is it, Canevin?" he inquired, helplessly.

I had had time to think during the consumption of that cigarette on the gallery. I had expected some such direct inquiry as this, and had my answer ready.

"There is no danger—nothing whatever to worry yourself about just now, at any rate," said I, with a positive finality which I was far from feeling internally. I was still shaken by what I had seen in that airy bedroom. "The ladies will be down shortly. We can not talk before them.

Besides, the fire may, possibly, be dangerous. I will tell you everything I know tomorrow morning. Come to my house at nine, if you please, sir."

The old Colonel showed his army training at this.

"Very well, Mr. Canevin," said he, "at nine tomorrow, at your house."

Lieutenant Farnum and his efficient direction proved too much for the fire. Within a half-hour or so, as we sat on the gallery, the ladies wearing shawls because of the cool breeze, my house-boy, Stephen, came to report to me that the fire was totally extinguished. We had seen none of its original glare for the past quarter of an hour. I said goodnight, and the Lorriquer family retired to make up its interrupted sleep, while I walked up the hill and around the corner to my own house and turned in. The only persons among us all who had not been disturbed that eventful night were Mrs. Preston's two small children. As it would be a simple matter to take them to safety in case the fire menaced the house, we had agreed to leave them as they were, and they had slept quietly throughout all our alarms and excursions!

The old Colonel looked his full seventy years the next morning when he arrived at my house and was shown out upon the gallery by Stephen, where I awaited him. His face was strained, lined, and ghastly.

"I did not sleep at all the rest of the night, Mr. Canevin," he confessed, "and four or five times I went to thy wife's room and looked in, but every time she was sleeping naturally. What do you make of the this dreadful happening, sir? I really do not know which way to turn, I admit to you, sir." The poor old man was in a truly pathetic state. I did what I could to reassure him.

I set out before him the whole case, as I have already set it out, as the details came before me, throughout the course of this narrative. I went into all the details, sparing nothing, even the delicate matter of Mrs Lorriquer's conduct over the card-table. Summing up the matter I said:

"It seems plain, from all this testimony, that Simon Legrand's haunting of his old house which you occupied for three years was more of an actuality than your residence there indicated to you. His sudden death at the hands of one of his 'guests' may very well have left his personality, perhaps fortified by some unfulfilled wish, about the premises which had been his for a number of years previously. There are many recorded cases of similar nature in the annals of scientific occult investigation. Such a 'shade,' animated by some compelling motive to persist in its earthly existence, would 'pervade' such premises already *en rapport* with his ways and customs." Then, for the first time, the old house was refurbished and occupied when you moved into it. Mrs. Lorriquer may be, doubtless is, I should suppose from the evidence we already have, one of those persons who is open to what seems to have happened to her. You mentioned her mother, a well-known medium of years ago. Such qualifications may well be more or less hereditary, you see.

"That Legrand laid hold upon the opportunity to manifest himself *through her,* we already know. Both of us have seen him, 'manifested' and in a manner typical of mediumistic productions, in material form, of their 'controls.' In this case, the degree of 'control' must be very strong, and, besides that, it has, plainly, been growing. The use of French, unconsciously, the very tone of his deep bass voice, also unconscious on her part, and—I will go farther, Colonel; there is another, and a very salient clue for us to use. You spoke of the fact that previous to your occupancy of the Legrand house in the 'zone' Mrs. Lorriquer never played cards. Obviously, if the rest of my inferences are correct, this desire to play cards came direct from Legrand, who was using her for his own self-expression, having, in some way, got himself *en rapport,* with her as her 'control.' I would go on, then, and hazard the guess that just as her use of French is plainly subconscious, as is the use of Legrand's voice, on occasion—you will remember, I spoke to him before you came into the room last night, *and he answered me in that same deep voice*— so her actual playing of cards is an act totally unconscious on her part, or nearly so. It is a wide sweep of the imagination, but, I think, it will be substantiated after we have released her from this obsession, occupation by another personality, or whatever it proves to be."The word "release" seemed to electrify the old gentleman. He jumped out of his chair, came toward me, his lined face alight with hope.

"Is there any remedy, Mr. Canevin? Can it be possible? Tell me, for God's sake, you can not understand how I am suffering—my poor wife! You have had much experience with this sort of thing; I, none whatever. It has always seemed—well, to put it bluntly, a lot of 'fake' to me."

"Yes," said I, slowly, "there is a remedy, Colonel—two remedies, in fact. The phenomenon with which we are confronted seems a kind of combination of mediumistic projection of the 'control,' and plain, old-fashioned 'possession.' The Bible, as you will recall, is full of such cases—the Cadarene Demoniac, for example. So, indeed, is the ecclesiastical history through the Middle Ages. Indeed, as you may be aware, the 'order' of exorcist still persists in at least one of the great historic churches. One remedy, then, is exorcism. It is unusual, these days, but I am myself familiar with two cases where it has been successfully performed, in Boston, Massachusetts, within the last decade. A salient point, if we should resort to that, however, is Mrs. Lorriquer's own religion. Exorcism can not, according to the rules, be accorded to everybody. The bare minimum is that the subject should be validly baptized. Otherwise exorcism is inoperative; it does not work as we understand its mystical or spiritual processes."

"Mrs. Lorriquer's family were all Friends—Quakers," said the Colonel. "She is not, to my knowledge, baptized. Her kind of Quakers do not, I believe, practise baptism."

"Well, then," said I, "there is another way, and that, with your permission, Colonel, I will outline to you."

"I am prepared to do anything, anything whatever, Mr. Canevin, to cure this horrible thing for my poor wife. The matter I leave entirely in your hands, and I will cooperate in every way, precisely as you say."

"Well said sir!" I exclaimed, and forthwith proceeded to outline my plan to the Colonel....

Perhaps there are some who would accuse me of being superstitious. As to that I do not know, and, quite frankly, I care little. However, I record that that afternoon I called on the rector of my own church in St. Thomas, the English Church, as the native people still call it, although it is no longer, now that St. Thomas is American territory, under the control of the Archbishop of the British West Indies as it was before our purchase from Denmark in 1917. I found the rector at home and proffered my request. It was for a vial of holy water. The rector and I walked across the street to the church and there in the sacristy, without comment, the good gentleman, an other-worldly soul much beloved by his congregation, provided my need. I handed him a twenty-franc note, for his poor, and took my departure, the bottle in the pocket of my white drill coat.

That evening, by arrangement with the Colonel, we gathered for an evening of cards at the Lorriquers'. I have never seen Mrs. Lorriquer more typically the termagant. She performed all her bag of tricks, such as I have recorded, and, shortly after eleven, when we had finished, Mrs. Preston's face wore a dull flush of annoyance and, when she retired, which she did immediately after we had calculated the final score, she hardly bade the rest of us goodnight.

Toward the end of the play, once more I happened to hold a commanding hand, and played it out to a successful five no-trump, bid and made. All through the process of playing that hand, adverse to Mrs. Lorriquer and her partner, I listened carefully to a monotonous, ill-natured kind of undertone chant with which she punctuated her obvious annoyance. What she was saying was:

"Nom de nom, de nom, de nom, de nom—" precisely as a testy, old-fashioned, grumbling Frenchman will repeat those nearly meaningless syllables.Mrs. Lorriquer retired not long after her daughter's departure upstairs, leaving the Colonel and me over a pair of Havana cigars.

We waited, according to our prearranged plan, down- stairs there, until one o'clock in the morning.

Then the Colonel, at my request, brought from the small room which he used as an office or den, the longer of a very beautiful pair of Samurai swords, a magnificent weapon, with a blade as keen and smooth as any razor. Upon this, with a clean hankerchief, I rubbed half the contents of my holy water, not only upon the shimmering, inlaid, beautiful blade, but over the hand-grip as well.

Shortly after one, we proceeded, very softly, upstairs, and straight to the door of Mrs. Lorriquer's room, where we took up our stand outside. We listened, and within there was no sound of any kind whatever.

From time to time the Colonel, stooping, would peer in through the large keyhole, designed for an enormous, old-fashioned, complicated key. After quite a long wait, at precisely twenty minutes before two a. m. the Colonel, straightening up again after such an inspection, nodded to me. His face, which had regained some of its wonted color during the day, was a ghastly white, quite suddenly, and his hands shook as he softly turned the handle of the door, opened it, and stood aside for me to enter, which I did, he following me, and closing the door behind him. Behind us, in the upper hallway, and just beside the door-jamb, we had left a large, strong wicker basket, the kind designed to hold a family washing.

Precisely as she had lain the night before, was Mrs. Lorriquer, on the huge four-poster. And, beside her, the stream of *plasma* flowing from her to him, stood Simon Legrand, glowering at us evilly. I advanced straight upon him, the beautiful knightly sword of Old Japan firmly held in my right hand, and as he shrank back, stretching the *plasma* stream to an extreme tenuity—like pulled dough it seemed—I abruptly cut through this softly-flowing material directly above the body of Mrs. Lorriquer with a transverse stroke. The sword met no apparent resistance as I did so, and then, without any delay, I turned directly upon Legrand, now muttering in a deep bass snarl, and with an accurately timed swing of the weapon, sheared off his head. At this stroke, the sword met resistance, comparable, perhaps, as nearly as I can express it, to the resistance which might be offered by the neck of a snow-man built by children. The head, bloodlessly, as I had anticipated, fell to the floor, landing with only a slight, *soft* sound, rolled a few feet, and came to a pause against the baseboard of the room. The decapitated body swayed and buckled toward my right, and, before it gave way completely and fell prone upon the bedroom floor, I had managed two more strokes, the first through the middle of the body, and the second a little above the knees. Then, as these large fragments lay upon the floor, I chopped them, lightly, into smaller sections.

As I made the first stroke, that just above Mrs. Lorriquer, severing the *plasma* stream, I heard from her a long, deep sound, like a sigh. Thereafter she lay quiet. There was no motion whatever from the sundered sections of "Simon Legrand" as these lay, quite inert, upon the floor, and, as I have indicated, no flow of blood from them. I turned to the Colonel, who stood just at my shoulder witnessing this extraordinary spectacle. "It worked out precisely as we anticipated," said I. "The horrible thing is over and done with, now. It is time for the next step."

The old Colonel nodded, and went to the door, which he opened, and through which he peered before stepping out into the hallway. Plainly we had made no noise. Mrs. Preston and her babies were asleep. The Colonel brought the clothes-basket into the room, and before us, the rather gingerly at first, we picked up the sections of what had been "Simon Legrand." They were surprizingly light, and, to the touch, felt somewhat like soft and pliant dough. Into the basket they went, all of them, and, carrying it between us—it seemed to weigh altogether no more than perhaps twenty pounds at the outside—we stepped softly out of the room, closing the door behind us, down the stairs, and out, through the dining-room and kitchen into the walled backyard.

Here, in the corner, stood the wire apparatus wherein papers and light trash were burned daily. Into this already half filled with various papers, the Colonel poured several quarts of kerosene from a large five-gallon container fetched from the kitchen, and upon this kindling we placed carefully the strange fragments from our clothes-basket. Then I set a match to it, and within ten minutes there remained nothing except small particles of unidentifiable trash, of the simulacrum of Simon Legrand.

We returned, softly, after putting back the kerosene and the clothes-basket where they belonged, into the house, closing the kitchen door after us. Again we mounted the stairs, and went into Mrs. Lorriquer's room. We walked over to the bed and looked at her. She seemed, somehow, shrunken, thinner than usual, less bulky, but, although there were deep, unaccustomed lines showing in her relaxed face, there was, too, upon that face, the very ghost of a kindly smile.

"It is just as you said it would be, Mr. Canevin," whispered the Colonel as we tiptoed down the stone stairway. I nodded.

"We will need an oiled rag for the sword," said I. "I wet it very thoroughly, you know."

"I will attend to that," said the Colonel, as he gripped my hand in a grasp of surprizing vigor.

"Good-night, sir," said I, and he accompanied me to the door.

The Colonel came in to see me about ten the next morning. I had only just finished a late "tea," as the early morning meal, after the Continental fashion, is still named in the Virgin Islands. The Colonel joined me at the table and took a late cup of coffee.

"I was sitting beside her when she awakened, a little before nine," he said, "and as she complained of an 'all-gone' feeling, I persuaded her to remain in bed, 'for a couple of days.' She was sleeping just now, very quietly and naturally, when I ran over to report."

I called the following morning to inquire for Mrs. Lorriquer. She was still in bed, and I left a polite message of good-will.

It was a full week before she felt well enough to get up, and it was two days after that that the Lorriquers invited me to dinner once more. The bulletins, surreptitiously reported to me by the Colonel, indicated that, as we had anticipated, she was slowly gaining strength. One of the Navy physicians, called in, had prescribed a mild tonic, which she had been taking.

The shrunken appearance persisted, I observed, but this, considering Mrs. Lorriquer's characteristic stoutness, was, actually, an improvement at least in her general appearance. The lines of her face appeared somewhat accentuated as compared to how she had looked before the last "manifestation" of the "control." Mrs. Preston seemed worried about her mother, but said little. She was rather unusually silent during dinner, I noticed.

I had one final test which I was anxious to apply. I waited for a complete pause in our conversation toward the end of a delightful dinner, served in Mrs. Lorriquer's best manner.

"And shall we have some Contract after dinner this evening?" I inquired, addressing Mrs. Lorriquer.

She almost blushed, looked at me deprecatingly.

"But, Mr. Canevin, you know—I know nothing of cards," she replied.

"Why, Mother!" exclaimed Mrs. Preston from across the table, and Mrs. Lorriquer looked at her in what seemed to be evident puzzlement. Mrs. Preston did not proceed, I suspect because her father touched her foot for silence under the table. Indeed, questioned, he admitted as much to me later that evening.

The old gentleman walked out with me, and half-way up the hall when I took my departure a little before eleven, after an evening of conservation punctuated by one statement of Mrs. Lorriquer's, made with a pleasant smile through a somewhat rueful face.

"Do you know, I've actually lost eighteen pounds, Mr. Canevin, and that being laid up in bed only eight or nine days. It seems incredible, does it not? The climate, perhaps——"

"Those scales must have been quite off," vouchsafed Mrs. Preston.

Going up the hill with the Colonel, I remarked:

"You still have one job on your hands, Colonel."

"Wh-what is that, Mr. Canevin?" inquired the old gentleman, apprehensively.

"Explaining the whole thing to your daughter," said I.

"I daresay it can be managed," returned Colonel Lorriquer. "I'll have a hack at that later!"

PASSING OF A GOD

"YOU say that when Carswell came into your hospital over in Port au Prince his fingers looked as though they had been wound with string," said I, encouragingly.

"It is a very ugly story, that, Canevin," replied Doctor Pelletier, still reluctant, it appeared.

"You promised to tell me," I threw in.

"I know it, Canevin," admitted Doctor Pelletier of the U. S. Navy Medical Corps, now stationed here in the Virgin Islands. "But," he proceeded, "you couldn't use this story, anyhow. There are editorial *tabus,* aren't there? The thing is too—what shall I say?—too outrageous, too incredible.""Yes." I admitted in turn, "there are *tabus,* plenty of them. Still, after hearing about those fingers, as though wound with string—why not give me the story, Pelletier; leave it to me whether or not I 'use' it. It's the story I want, mostly. I'm burning up for it!""I suppose it's your lookout," said my guest. "If you find it too gruesome for you, tell me and I'll quit."

I plucked up hope once more. I had been trying for this story, after getting little scraps of it which allured and intrigued me, for weeks.

"Start in," I ventured, soothingly, pushing the silver swizzel-jug after the humidor of cigarettes from which Pelletier was even now making a selection. Pelletier helped himself to the swizzel frowningly. Evidently he was torn between the desire to pour out the story of Arthur Carswell and some complication of feelings against doing so. I sat back in my wicker lounge-chair and waited.

Pelletier moved his large bulk about in his chair. Plainly now he was cogitating how to open the tale. He began, meditatively:

"I don't know as I ever heard public discussion of the malignant bodily growths except among medical people. Science knows little about them. The fact of such diseases, though, is well known to everybody, through campaigns of prevention, the life insurance companies, appeals for funds—

"Well, Carswell's case, primarily, is one of those cases."

He paused and gazed into the glowing end of his cigarette.

"'Primarily?'" I threw in encouragingly.

"Yes. Speaking as a surgeon, that's where this thing begins, I suppose."

I kept still, waiting.

"Have you read Seabrook's book, *The Magic island,* Canevin?" asked Pelletier suddenly."Yes," I answered. "What about it?"

"Then I suppose that from your own experience knocking around the West Indies and your study of it all, a good bit of that stuff of Seabrook's is familiar to you, isn't it?—the *vodu,* and the hill customs, and all the rest of it, especially over in Haiti—you could check up on a writer like Seabrook, couldn't you, more or less?""Yes," said I, "practically all of it was an old story to me—a very fine piece of work, however, the thing clicks all the way through—an honest and thorough piece of investigation."

"Anything in it new to you?"

"Yes—Seabrook's statement that there was an exchange of personalities between the sacrificial goat—at the 'baptism'—and the young Black girl, the chapter he calls: *Girl-Cry—Goat-Cry.* That, at least, was a new one on me, I admit.""You will recall, if you read it carefully, that he attributed that phenomenon to his own personal 'slant' on the thing. Isn't that the case, Canevin?"

"Yes," I agreed, "I think that is the way he put it."

"Then, resumed Doctor Pelletier, "I take it that all that material of his—I notice that there have been a lot of story-writers using his terms lately!—is sufficiently familiar to you so that you have some clear idea of the Haitian-African demigods, like Ogoun Badagris, Damballa, and the others, taking up their residence for a short time in some devotee?"

"The idea is very well understood," said I, "Mr. Sea brook mentions it among a number of other local phenomena. It was an old negro who came up to him while he was eating, thrust his soiled bands into the dishes of food, surprized him considerably—then was surrounded by worshippers who took him to the nearest *houmfort* or *vodu*-house, let him Sit on the altar, brought him food, hung all their jewelry on him, worshipped him for the time being; then, characteristically, quite utterly ignored the original old fellow after the 'possession' on the part of the 'deity' ceased and reduced him to an unimportant old pantaloon as he was before,""That summarizes it exactly," agreed Doctor Pelletier. "That, Canevin, that kind of thing, I mean, is the real starting-place of this dreadful matter of Arthur Carswell."

"You mean—?" I barged out at Pelletier, vastly intrigued. I had had no idea that there was *vodu* mixed in with the case."I mean that Arthur Carswell's first intimation that there was anything pressingly wrong with him was just such a 'possession' as the one you have recounted."

"But—but," I protested, "I had supposed—I had every reason to believe, that it was a surgical matter! Why, you just objected to telling about it on the ground that—"

"Precisely," said Doctor Pelletier, calmly. "It was such a surgical case, but, as I say, it *began* in much the same way as the 'occupation' of that old negro's body by Egon Badagris or whichever one of their devilish deities that happened to be, just as, you say, is well known to fellows like yourself who go in for such things, and just as Seabrook recorded it.""Well," said I, "you go ahead in your own way, Pelletier. I'll do my best to listen. Do you mind an occasional question?"

"Not in the least," said Doctor Pelletier considerately, shifted himself to a still more pronouncedly recumbent position in my Chinese rattan lounge-chair, lit a fresh cigarette, and proceeded:

"Carswell had worked up a considerable intimacy with the snake-worship of interior Haiti, all the sort of thing familiar to you; the sort of thing set out, probably for the first time in English at least, in Seabrook's book; all the gatherings, and the 'baptism,' and the sacrifices of the fowls and the bull, and the goats; the orgies of the worshippers, the boom and thrill of the *rata* drums—all that strange, incomprehensible, rather silly-surfaced, deadly-underneathed worship of 'the Snake' which the Dahomeyans brought with them to old Hispaniola, now Haiti and the Dominican Republic."He had been there, as you may have heard, for a number of years; went there in the first place because everybody thought he was a kind of failure at home; made a good living, too, in a way nobody but an original-minded fellow like him would have thought of—shot ducks on the Léogane marshes, dried them, and exported them to New York and San Francisco to the United States' two largest Chinatowns.

"For a 'failure,' too, Carswell was a particularly smart-looking chap, in the English sense of that word. He was one of those fellows who was always shaved, clean, freshly groomed, even under the rather adverse conditions of his living, there in Léogane by the salt marshes; and of his trade, which was to kill and dry ducks. A fellow can get pretty careless and let himself go at that sort of thing, away from 'home'; away, too, from such niceties as there are in a place like Port au Prince.

"He looked, in fact, like a fellow just off somebody's yacht the first time I saw him, there in the hospital in Port au Prince, and that, too, was right after a rather singular experience which would have unnerved or unsettled pretty nearly anybody.

"But not so old Carswell. No, indeed. I speak of him as 'Old Carswell,' Canevin. That, though, is a kind of affectionate term. He was somewhere about forty-five then; it was two years ago, you see, and, in addition to his being very spick and span, well groomed, you know, he looked surprizingly young, somehow. One of those faces which showed experience, but, along with the experience, a philosophy. The lines in his face were good lines, if you get what I mean—lines of humor and courage; no dissipation, no let-down kind of lines, nothing of slackness such as you would see in the face of even a comparatively young beach-comber. No, as he strode into my office, almost jauntily, there in the hospital, there was nothing, nothing whatever, about him, to suggest anything else but a prosperous fellow American, a professional chap, for choice, who might, as I say, have just come ashore from somebody's yacht.

"And yet—good God, Canevin, the story that came out—!"

Naval surgeon though he was, with service in Haiti, at sea, in Nicaragua, the China Station to his credit, Doctor Pelletier rose at this point, and, almost agitatedly, walked up and down my gallery. Then he sat down and lit a fresh cigarette.

"There is," he said, reflectively, and as though weighing his words carefully, "there is, Canevin, among various others, a somewhat 'wild' theory that somebody put forward several years ago, about the origin of malignant tumors. It never gained very much approval among the medical profession, but it has, at least, the merit of originality, and—it was new. Because of those facts, it had a certain amount of currency, and there are those, in and out of medicine, who still believe in it. It is that there are certain nuclei, certain masses, so to speak, of the bodily material which have persisted—not generally, you understand, but in certain cases—among certain persons, the kind who are 'susceptible' to this horrible disease, which, in the prenatal state, did not develop fully or normally—little places in the bodily structure, that is—if I make myself clear?—which remain undeveloped.

"Something, according to this hypothesis, something like a sudden jar, or a bruise, a kick, a blow with the fist, the result of a fall, or whatnot, causes traumatism—physical injury, that is, you know—to one of the focus-places, and the undeveloped little mass of material starts in to grow, and so displaces the normal tissue which surrounds it.

"One objection to the theory is that there are at least two varieties, well-known and recognized scientifically; the carcinoma, which is itself subdivided into two kinds, the hard and the soft carcinomae, and the sarcoma, which is a soft thing, like what is popularly understood by a 'tumor.' Of course they are all 'tumors,' particular kinds of tumors, malignant tumors. What lends a certain credibility to the theory I have just mentioned is the malignancy, the growing element. For, whatever the underlying reason, they grow, Canevin, as is well recognized, and this explanation I have been talking about gives a reason for the growth. The 'malignancy' is, really, that one of the things seems to have, as it were, its own life. All this, probably. you know?"

I nodded. I did not wish to interrupt. I could see that this side-issue on a scientific by-path must have something to do with the story of Carswell.

"Now," resumed Pelletier, "notice this fact, Canevin. Let me put it in the form of a question, like this: To what kind, or type, of *vodu*worshipper, does the 'possession' by one of their deities occur—from your own knowledge of such things, what would you say?""To the incomplete; the abnormal, to an old man, or woman," said I, slowly, reflecting, "or—to a child, or, perhaps, to an idiot. Idiots, ancient crones, backward children, 'town-fools' and the like, all over Europe, are supposed to be in some mysterious way *en rapport* with deity—or with Satan! It is an established peasant belief. Even among the Mahometans, the moron or idiot is 'the afflicted of God.' There is no other better established belief along such lines of thought.""Precisely!" exclaimed Pelletier, "and, Canevin, go back once more to Seabrook's instance that we spoke about. What type of person was 'possessed'?"

"An old doddering man," said I, "one well gone in his dotage apparently."

"Right once more! Note now, two things. First, I will admit to you, Canevin, that that theory I have just been expounding never made much of a hit with me. It might be true, but—very few first-rate men in our profession thought much of it, and I followed that negative lead and didn't think much of it, or, indeed, much about it. I put it down to the vaporings of the theorist who first thought it out and published it, and let it go at that. Now, Canevin, *I am convinced that it is true!* The second thing, then: When Carswell came into my office in the hospital over there in Port an Prince, the first thing I noticed about him—I had never seen him before, you see—was a peculiar, almost an indescribable, discrepancy. It was between his general appearance of weather-worn cleanliness, general fitness, his 'smart' appearance in his clothes—all that, which fitted together about the clean-cut, open character of the fellow; and what I can only describe as a pursiness. He seemed in good condition, I mean to say, and yet—there was something, somehow, *flabby* somewhere in his makeup. I couldn't put my finger on it, but—it was there, a suggestion of something that detracted from the impression he gave as being an upstanding fellow, a good-fellow-to-have-beside-you-in-a-pinch—that kind of person."The second thing I noticed, it was just after he had taken a chair beside my desk, was his fingers, and thumbs. They were swollen, Canevin, looked sore, as though they had been wound with string. That was the first thing I thought of, being wound with string. He saw me looking at them, held them out to me abruptly, laid them side by side, his hands I mean, on my desk, and smiled at me.

e you have noticed them, Doctor,' he remarked, almost jovi-
it makes it a little easier for me to tell you what I'm here for.
ll, you might put it down as a "symptom."'

oked at his fingers and thumbs; every one of them was affected
in the same way; and ended up with putting a magnifying glass over
them.

"They were all bruised and reddened, and here and there on several of them, the skin was abraded, broken, circularly—it was a most
curious-looking set of digits. My new patient was addressing me again:

"I'm not here to ask you riddles, Doctor,' he said, gravely, this time,
'but—would you care to make a guess at what did that to those fingers
and thumbs of mine?'

"'Well,' I came back at him, 'without knowing what's happened,
it *looks* as if you'd been trying to wear about a hundred rings, all at one
time, and most of them didn't fit!'"Carswell nodded his head at me.
'Score one for the medico,' said he, and laughed. 'Even numerically
you're almost on the dot, sir. The precise number was one hundred and
six!'

"I confess, I stared at him then. But he wasn't fooling. It was a cold,
sober, serious fact that he was stating; only, he saw that it had a humorous side, and that intrigued him, as anything humorous always did, I
found out after I got to know Carswell a lot better than I did then."

"You said you wouldn't mind a few questions, Pelletier," I inter-
jected.

"Fire away," said Pelletier. "Do you see any light, so far?"

"I was naturally figuring along with you, as you told about it all,"
said I. "Do I infer correctly that Carswell, having lived there-how long,
four or five years or so?—"

"Seven, to be exact," put in Pelletier.

"—that Carswell, being pretty familiar with the native doings, had
mixed into things, got the confidence of his Black neighbors in and
around Léogane, become somewhat 'adept,' had the run of the *houm-
forts,* so to speak— *'votre bougie, M'sieu'*—the fortune-telling at the fes-
tivals, and so forth, and—had been 'visited' by one of the Black deities?
That, apparently, if I'm any judge of tendencies, is what your account
seems to be leading up to. Those bruised fingers—the one hundred and
six rings—good heavens, man, is it really possible?""Carswell told me
all about that end of it, a little later—yes, that was, precisely, what happened, but—that surprizing, incredible as it seems, is only the small end
of it all. You just wait—"

"Go ahead," said I, "I am all ears, I assure you!"

"Well, Carswell took his hands off the desk after I had looked at them through my magnifying glass, and then waved one of them at me in a kind of deprecating gesture.

"'I'll go into all that, if you're interested to hear about it, Doctor,' he assured me, 'but that isn't what I'm here about. His face grew suddenly very grave. 'Have you plenty of time?' he asked. 'I don't want to let my case interfere with anything.'

"'Fire ahead,' says I, and he leaned forward in his chair.

"'Doctor,' says he, 'I don't know whether or not you ever heard of me before. My name's Carswell, and I live over Léogane way. I'm an American, like yourself, as you can probably see, and, even after seven years of it, out there, duck-hunting, mostly, with virtually no White-man's doings for a pretty long time, I haven't "gone native" or anything of the sort. I wouldn't want you to think I'm one of those wasters.' He looked up at me inquiringly for my estimate of him. He had been by himself a good deal; perhaps too much. I nodded at him. He looked me in the eye, squarely, and nodded back. 'I guess we understand each other,' he said. Then he went on.

"'Seven years ago, it was, I came down here. I've lived over there ever since. What few people know about me regard me as a kind of fail-ure, I daresay. But—Doctor, there was a reason for that, a pretty definite reason. I won't go into it beyond your end of it—the medical end, I mean. I came down because of this.'

"He stood up then, and I saw what made that 'discrepancy' I spoke about, that 'flabbiness' which went so ill with the general cut of the man. He turned up the lower ends of his white drill jacket and put his hand a little to the left of the middle of his stomach. 'Just notice this,' he said, and stepped toward me.

"There, just over the left center of that area and extending up toward the spleen, on the left side, you know, there was a protuberance. Seen closely it was apparent that here was some sort of internal growth. It was that which had made him look flabby, stomachish.

"'This was diagnosed for me in New York,' Carswell explained, 'a little more than seven years ago. They told me it was inoperable then. After seven years, probably, I daresay it's worse, if anything. To put the thing in a nutshell, Doctor, I had to "let go" then. I got out of a promising business, broke off my engagement, came here. I won't expatiate on it all, but—it was pretty tough, Doctor, pretty tough. I've lasted all right, so far. It hasn't troubled me—until just lately. That's why I drove in this afternoon, to see you, to see if anything could be done.'

"'Has it been kicking up lately?' I asked him.

"'Yes,' said Carswell, simply. 'They said it would kill me, probably within a year or so, as it grew. It hasn't grown—much. I've lasted a little more than seven years, so far.'

"'Come in to the operating-room,' I invited him, 'and take your clothes off, and let's get a good look at it.'

"'Anything you say,' returned Carswell, and followed me back into the operating-room then and there.

"I had a good look at Carswell, first, superficially. That preliminary examination revealed a growth quite typical, the self-contained, not the 'fibrous' type, in the location I've already described, and about the size of an average man's head. It lay imbedded, fairly deep. It was what we call 'encapsulated.' That, of course, is what had kept Carswell alive.

"Then we put the X-rays on it, fore-and-aft, and sidewise. One of those things doesn't always respond very well to skiagraphic examination, to the X-ray, that is, but this one showed clearly enough. Inside it appeared a kind of dark, triangular mass, with the small end at the top. When Doctor Smithson and I had looked him over thoroughly, I asked Carswell whether or not he wanted to stay with us, to come into the hospital as a patient, for treatment.

"'I'm quite in your hands, Doctor,' he told me. 'I'll stay, or do whatever you want me to. But, first,' and for the first time he looked a trifle embarrassed, 'I think I'd better tell you the story that goes with my coming here! However, speaking plainly, do you think I have a chance?'

"Well,' said I, 'speaking plainly, yes, there is a chance, maybe a "fifty-fifty" chance, maybe a little less. On the one hand, this thing has been let alone for seven years since original diagnosis. It's probably less operable than it was when you were in New York. On the other hand, we know a lot more, not about these things, Mr. Carswell, but about surgical technique, than they did seven years ago. On the whole, I'd advise you to stay and get ready for an operation, and, say about "forty-sixty" you'll go back to Léogane, or back to New York if you feel like it, several pounds lighter in weight and a new man. If it takes you, on the table, well, you've had a lot more time out there gunning for ducks in Léogane than those New York fellows allowed you.'

"I'm with you,' said Carswell, and we assigned him a room, took his 'history,' and began to get him ready for his operation.

"We did the operation two days later, at ten-thirty in the morning, and in the meantime Carswell told me his 'story' about it.

"It seems that he had made quite a place for himself, there in Léogane, among the negroes and the ducks. In seven years a man like Carswell, with his mental and dispositional equipment, can go quite a long way, anywhere. He had managed to make quite a good thing out of his duck-drying industry, employed five or six 'hands' in his little wooden 'factory,' rebuilt a rather good house he had secured there for a song right after he had arrived, collected local antiques to add to the equipment he had brought along with him, made himself a real home of a peculiar, bachelor kind, and, above all, got in solid with the Black People all around him. Almost incidentally I gathered from him—he had no gift of narrative, and I had to question him a great deal—he had got onto, and into, the know in the *vodu* thing. There wasn't, as far as I could get it, any aspect of it all that he hadn't been in on, except, that is, *'la chevre sans cornes'*—the goat without horns, you know—the human sacrifice on great occasions. In fact, he strenuously denied that the *voduists* resorted to that; said it was a canard against them; that they never, really, did such things, never had, unless back in prehistoric times, in Guinea—Africa."But, there wasn't anything about it all that he hadn't at his very finger ends, and at first-hand, too. The man was a walking encyclopedia of the native beliefs, customs, and practises. He knew, too, every turn and twist of their speech. He hadn't, as he had said at first, 'gone native' in the slightest degree, and yet, without lowering his White Man's dignity by a trifle, he had got it all.

"That brings us to the specific happening, the 'story' which, he had said, went along with his reason for coming in to the hospital in Port au Prince, to us.

"It appears that his sarcoma had never, practically, troubled. Beyond noting a very gradual increase in its size from year to year, he said, he 'wouldn't know he had one.' In other words, characteristically, it never gave him any pain or direct annoyance beyond the sense of the wretched thing being there, and increasing on him, and always drawing him closer to that end of life which the New York doctors had warned him about.

"Then, it had happened only three days before he came to the hospital, he had gone suddenly unconscious one afternoon, as he was walking down his shell path to his gateway. The last thing he remembered then was being 'about four steps from the gate.' When he woke up, it was dark. He was seated in a big chair on his own front gallery, and the first thing he noticed was that his fingers and thumbs were sore and ached very painfully. The next thing was that there were flares burning all along the edge of the gallery, and down in the front yard, and along the road outside the paling fence that divided his property from the road, and in the light of these flares, there swarmed literally hundreds of negroes, gathered about him and mostly on their knees; lined along the gallery and on the grounds below it; prostrating themselves, chanting, putting earth and sand on their heads; and, when he leaned back in his chair, something hurt the back of his neck, and he found that he was being nearly choked with the necklaces, strings of beads, gold and silver coin-strings, and other kinds, that had been draped over his head. His fingers, and the thumbs as well, were covered with gold and silver rings, many of them jammed on so as to stop the circulation.

"From his knowledge of their beliefs, he recognized what had happened to him. He had, he figured, probably fainted, although such a thing was not at all common with him, going down the pathway to the yard gate, and the Blacks had supposed him to be 'possessed' as he had several times seen Black people, children, old men and women, morons, chiefly, similarly 'possessed.' He knew that, now that he was recovered from whatever had happened to him, the 'worship' ought to cease and if he simply sat quiet and took what was coming to him, they would, as soon as they realized he was 'himself' once more, leave him alone and he would get some relief from this uncomfortable set of surroundings; get rid of the necklaces and the rings; get a little privacy.

"But—the queer part of it all was that they didn't quit. No, the mob around the house and on the gallery increased rather than diminished, and at last he was put to it, from sheer discomfort—he said he came to the point where he felt he couldn't stand it all another instant—to speak up and ask the people to leave him in peace.

"They left him, he says, at that, right off the bat, immediately, without a protesting voice, but—and here was what started him on his major puzzlement—they didn't take off the necklaces and rings. No—they left the whole set of that metallic drapery which they had hung and thrust upon him right there, and, after he had been left alone, as he had requested, and had gone into his house, and lifted off the necklaces and worked the rings loose, the next thing that happened was that old Pa'p Josef, the local *papaloi,* together with three or four other neighboring *papalois,* witch-doctors from nearby villages, and followed by a very old man who was known to Carswell as the *hougon,* or head witch-doctor of the whole countryside thereabouts, came in to him in a kind of procession, and knelt down all around him on the floor of his living-room, and laid down gourds of cream and bottles of red rum and cooked chickens, and even a big china bowl of Tannia soup—a dish he abominated, said it always tasted like soapy water to him!—and then backed out leaving him to these comestibles."He said that this sort of attention persisted in his case, right through the three days that he remained in his house in Léogane, before he started out for the hospital; would, apparently, be still going on if he hadn't come in to Port au Prince to us.

"But—his coming in was not, in the least, because of this. It had puzzled him a great deal, for there was nothing like it in his experience, nor, so far as he could gather from their attitude, in the experience of the people about him, of the *papalois,* or even of the*hougan* himself. They acted, in other words, precisely as though the 'deity' supposed to have taken up his abode within him had remained there, although there seemed no precedent for such an occurrence, and, so far as he knew, he felt precisely just as he had felt right along, that is, fully awake, and, certainly, not in anything like an abnormal condition, and, very positively, not in anything like a fainting-fit!"That is to say—he felt precisely the same as usual except that—he attributed it to the probability that he must have fallen on the ground that time when he lost consciousness going down the pathway to the gate (he had been told that passers-by had picked him up and carried him to the gallery where he had awakened, later, these Good Samaritans meanwhile recognizing that one of the 'deities' had indwelt him)—he felt the same except for recurrent, almost unbearable pains in the vicinity of his lower abdominal region.

"There was nothing surprising to him in this accession of the new painfulness. He had been warned that that would be the beginning of the end. It was in the rather faint hope that something might be done that he had come in to the hospital. It speaks volumes for the man's fortitude, for his strength of character, that he came in so cheerfully; acquiesced in what we suggested to him to do; remained with us, facing those comparatively slim chances with complete cheerfulness.

"For—we did not deceive Carswell—the chances were somewhat slim. 'Sixty-forty' I had said, but as I afterward made clear to him, the favorable chances, as gleaned from the mortality tables, were a good deal less than that.

"He went to the table in a state of mind quite unchanged from his accustomed cheerfulness. He shook hands good-bye with Doctor Smithson and me, 'in case,' and also with Doctor Jackson, who acted as anesthetist.

"Carswell took an enormous amount of ether to get him off. His consciousness persisted longer, perhaps, than that of any surgical patient I can remember. At last, however, Doctor Jackson intimated to me that I might begin, and, Doctor Smithson standing by with the retracting forceps, I made the first incision It was my intention, after careful study of the X-ray plates, to open it up from in front, in an up-and-down direction, establish drainage directly, and, leaving the wound in the sound tissue in front of it open, to attempt to get it healed up after removing its contents. Such is the technique of the major portion of successful operations.

"It was a comparatively simple matter to expose the outer wall. This accomplished, and after a few words of consultation with my colleague, I very carefully opened it. We recalled that the X-ray had shown, as I mentioned, a triangular-shaped mass within. This apparent content we attributed to some obscure chemical coloration of the contents. I made my incisions with the greatest care and delicacy, of course. The critical part of the operation lay right at this point, and the greatest exactitude was indicated, of course.

"At last the outer coats of it were cut through, and retracted, and with renewed caution I made the incision through the inmost wall of tissue. To my surprise, and to Doctor Smithson's, the inside was comparatively dry. The gauze which the nurse attending had caused to follow the path of the knife, was hardly moistened. I ran my knife down below the original scope of the last incision, then upward from its upper extremity, greatly lengthening the incision as a whole, if you are following me.

"Then, reaching my gloved hand within this long up- and-down aperture, I felt about and at once discovered that I could get my fingers in around the inner containing wall quite easily. I reached and worked my fingers in farther and farther, finally getting both hands inside and at last feeling my fingers touch inside the posterior or rear wall. Rapidly, now, I ran the edges of my hands around inside, and, quite easily, lifted out the 'inside.' This, a mass weighing several pounds, of more or less solid material, was laid aside on the small table beside the operating-table, and, again pausing to consult with Doctor Smithson—the operation was going, you see, a lot better than either of us had dared to anticipate—and being encouraged by him to proceed to a radical step which we had not hoped to be able to take, I began the dissection from the surrounding, normal tissue, of the now collapsed walls. This, a long, difficult, and harassing job, was accomplished at the end of, perhaps, ten or twelve minutes of gruelling work, and the bag-like thing, now completely severed from the tissues in which it had been for so long imbedded, was placed also on the side table.

"Doctor Jackson reporting favorably on our patient's condition under the anesthetic, I now proceeded to dress the large aperture, and to close the body-wound. This was accomplished in a routine manner, and then, together, we bandaged Carswell, and he was taken back to his room to await awakening from the ether.

"Carswell disposed of, Doctor Jackson and Doctor Smithson left the operating-room and the nurse started in cleaning up after the operation; dropping the instruments into the boiler, and so on—a routine set of duties. As for me, I picked up the shell in a pair of forceps, turned it about under the strong electric operating-light, and laid it down again. It presented nothing of interest for a possible laboratory examination.

"Then I picked up the more or less solid contents which I had laid, very hastily, and without looking at it—you see, my actual removal of it had been done inside, in the dark for the most part and by the sense of feeling, with my hands, you will remember—I picked it up; I still had my operating-gloves on to prevent infection when looking over these specimens, and, still, not looking at it particularly, carried it out into the laboratory.

"Canevin"—Doctor Pelletier looked at me somberly through the very gradually fading light of late afternoon, the period just before the abrupt falling of our tropic dusk—"Canevin," he repeated, "honestly, I don't know how to tell you! Listen now,, old man, do something for me, will you?"

"Why, yes—of course," said I, considerably mystified. "What is it you want me to do, Pelletier?"

"My car is out in front of the house. Come on home with me, up to my house, will you? Let's say I want to give you a cocktail! Anyhow, maybe you'll understand better when you are there, *I want to tell you the rest up at my house, not here.* Will you please come, Canevin?"I looked at him closely. This seemed to me a very strange, an abrupt, request. Still, there was nothing whatever unreasonable about such a sudden whim on Pelletier's part.

"Why, yes, certainly I'll go with you, Pelletier, if you want me to."

"Come on, then," said Pelletier, and we started for his car.

The doctor drove himself, and after we had taken the first turn in the rather complicated route from my house to his, on the extreme airy top of Denmark Hill, he said, in a quiet voice:

"Put together, now, Canevin, certain points, if you please, in this story. Note, kindly, how the Black people over in Léogane acted, according to Carswell's story. Note, too, that theory I was telling you about; do you recollect it clearly?"

"Yes," said I, still more mystified.

"Just keep those two points in mind, then," added Doctor Pelletier, and devoted himself to navigating sharp turns and plodding up two steep roadways for the rest of the drive to his house.

We went in and found his houseboy laying the table for his dinner. Doctor Pelletier is unmarried, keeps a hospitable bachelor establishment. He ordered cocktails, and the houseboy departed on this errand. Then he led me into a kind of office, littered with medical and surgical paraphernalia. He lifted some papers off a chair, motioned me into it, and took another near by. "Listen, now!" he said, and held up a finger at me.

"I took that thing, as I mentioned, into the laboratory," said he. "I carried it in my hand, with my gloves still on, as aforesaid. I laid it down on a table and turned on a powerful light over it. It was only then that

I took a good look at it. It weighed several pounds at least, was about the bulk and heft of a full-grown coconut, and about the same color as a hulled coconut, that is, a kind of medium brown. As I looked at it, I saw that it was, as the -ray had indicated, vaguely triangular in shape. It lay over on one of its sides under that powerful light, and—Canevin, so help me God"—Doctor Pelletier leaned toward me, his face working, a great seriousness in his eyes—"it moved, Canevin," he murmured; "and, as I looked-the thing *breathed!* I was just plain dumbfounded. A biological specimen like that—does not move, Canevin! I shook all over, suddenly. I felt my hair prickle on the roots of my scalp. I felt chills go down my spine. Then I remembered that here I was, after an operation, in my own biological laboratory. I came close to the thing and propped it up, on what might be called its logical base, if you see what I mean, so that it stood as nearly upright as its triangular conformation permitted."And then I saw that it had faint yellowish markings over the brown, and that what you might call its skin was moving, and—as I stared at the thing, Canevin—two things like little arms began to move, and the top of it gave a kind of convulsive shudder, and it opened straight at me, Canevin, a pair of eyes and looked me in the face.

"Those eyes—my God, Canevin, those eyes! They were eyes of something more than human, Canevin, something incredibly evil, something vastly old, sophisticated, cold, immune from anything except pure evil, the eyes of something that had been worshipped, Canevin, from ages and ages out of a past that went back before all known human calculation. eyes that showed all the deliberate, lurking wickedness that has ever been in the world. The eyes closed, Canevin, and the thing sank over onto its side, and heaved and shuddered convulsively.

It was sick, Canevin; and now, emboldened, holding myself together. repeating over and over to myself that I had a case of the quavers, of post-operative 'nerves.' I forced myself to look closer, and as I did so I got from it a faint whiff of ether. Two tiny, ape-like nostrils, over a clamped-shut slit of a mouth. were exhaling and inhaling, drawing in the good. pure air, exhaling ether fumes. It popped into my head that Carswell bad consumed a terrific amount of ether before he went under; we had commented on that, Doctor Jackson particularly. I put two and two together, Canevin, remembered we were in Haiti, where things are not like New York; or Boston, or Baltimore! Those negroes had believed that the 'deity' had not come out of Carswell, do you see? That was the thing that held the edge of my mind. The thing stirred uneasily, put out one of its 'arms.' groped about, stiffened."I reached for a near-by specimen-jar, Canevin, reasoning, almost blindly, that if this thing were susceptible to ether, it would be susceptible to—well, my gloves were still on my hands, and—now shuddering so that I could hardly move at all, I had to force every motion—I reached out and took hold of the thing—it felt like moist leather—and dropped it into the jar. Then I carried the carboy of preserving alcohol over to the table and poured it in till the ghastly thing was entirely covered, the alcohol near the top of the jar. It writhed once, then rolled over on its 'back,' and lay still, the mouth now open. Do you believe me, Canevin?"

"I have always said that I would believe anything, on proper evidence," said I, slowly, "and I would be the last to question a statement of yours, Pelletier. However, although I have, as you say, looked into some of these things perhaps more than most, it seems, well—"

Doctor Pelletier said nothing. Then he slowly got up out of his chair. He stepped over to a wall-cupboard and returned, a wide-mouthed specimen-jar in his hand. He laid the jar down before me, in silence.

I looked into it, through the slightly discolored alcohol with which the jar, tightly sealed with rubber-tape and sealing-wax, was filled nearly to the brim. There, on the jar's bottom, lay such a thing as Pelletier had described (a thing which, if it had been "seated," upright would somewhat have resembled that representation of the happy little godling "Billiken" which was popular twenty years ago as a desk ornament), a thing suggesting the sinister, the unearthly, even in this desiccated form. I looked long at the thing.

"Excuse me for even seeming to hesitate, Pelletier," said I, reflectively.

"I can't say that I blame you," returned the genial doctor. "It is, by the way, the first and only time I have ever tried to tell the story to anybody."

"And Carswell?" I asked. "I've been intrigued with that good fellow and his difficulties. How did he come out of it all?"

"He made a magnificent recovery from the operation," said Pelletier, "and afterward, when he went back to Léogane, he told me that the negroes. while glad to see him quite usual, had quite lost interest in him as the throne of a 'divinity'."

"H'm," I remarked, "it would seem, that, to bear out—"

"Yes," said Pelletier, "I have always regarded that fact as absolutely conclusive. Indeed, how otherwise could one possibly account for—this?" He indicated the contents of the laboratory jar.

I nodded my head, in agreement with him. "I can only say that—if you won't feel insulted, Pelletier—that you are singularly open-minded, for a man of science! What, by the way, became of Carswell?"

The houseboy came in with a tray, and Pelletier and I drank to each other's good health.

"He came in to Port au Prince," replied Pelletier after he had done the honors. "He did not want to go back to the States, he said. The lady to whom he had been engaged had died a couple of years before; he felt that he would be out of touch with American business. The fact is—he had stayed out here too long, too continuously. But, he remains an 'authority' on Haitian native affairs, and is consulted by the High Commissioner. He knows, literally, more about Haiti than the Haitians themselves. I wish you might meet him; you'd have a lot in common."

"I'll hope to do that," said I, and rose to leave. The house-boy appeared at the door, smiling in my direction.

"The table is set for two, sar," said he.

Doctor Pelletier led the way into the dining-room, taking it for granted that I would remain and dine with him. We are informal in St. Thomas, about such matters. I telephoned home and sat down with him.

Pelletier suddenly laughed—he was half-way through his soup at the moment. I looked up inquiringly. He put down his soup spoon and looked across the table at me.

"It's a bit odd," he remarked, "when you stop to think of it! There's one thing Carswell doesn't know about Haiti and what happens there!"

"What's that?" I inquired.

"That—thing—in there," said Pelletier, indicating the office with his thumb in the way artists and surgeons do. "I thought he'd had troubles enough without *that* on his mind, too."I nodded in agreement and resumed my soup. Pelletier has a cook in a thousand.

HILL DRUMS

WHEN Mr. William Palgrave, British consul-general at St. Thomas, Danish West Indies, stepped out of his fine residence on Denmark Hill, he looked, as one local wit had unkindly remarked, "like an entire procession!" It could not be denied that handsome Mr. Palgrave, diplomat, famed author of travel articles in the leading British magazines, made at all times a vastly imposing appearance, and that of this appearance he was entirely conscious.

One blazing afternoon in May, in the year of Grace, 1873, he came statelily down the steps before his house toward his open carriage, waiting in the roadway below. On the box Claude, his negro coachman, sagged down now under the broiling sun, conversed languidly with one La Touche Penn, a street loafer whose swart skin showed through various rents in a faded, many-times-washed blue dungaree shirt. Seeing the consul-general descending, Claude straightened himself abruptly while La Touche Penn slouched away, the white of an observant, rolled eye on Mr. Palgrave.

As this ne'er-do-well strolled nonchalantly down the hill—the hard soles of a pair of feet which had never known the constriction of shoes making sandpaper-like sounds on the steep roadway—he whistled, softly, a nearly soundless little tune. Claude tightened his reins and the small, grass-fed, somnolent carriage-horses plucked up weary heads, ending their nap in the drowsy air. That was how Mr. Palgrave liked to find his appointments—in order; ready for their functions. Mr. Palgrave—so another St. Thomas wit—was not unlike the late General Braddock whose fame is in the American histories; in short, a bureaucratic martinet whose wide travels, soon to bring him greater fame as the distinguished author of *Ulysses,* had failed signally to modify a native phlegmatic bluntness.He came down the steps, a resplendent figure of a fine gentleman, dressed with a precise meticulousness in the exact mode of the London fashion, and, glancing after the furtive wastrel now well down the hill road, he caught the whistled tune. As he recognized it he frowned heavily, pursing his lips into a kind of pout which went ill with his appearance of portly, well-nourished grandeur. This accomplished diplomat was fastidious, easily annoyed. Not to put too fine a point upon it, he did not like St. Thomas.

For one thing he disliked feminine names for places, and the capital town in those days was called Charlotte Amalia, after one of Denmark's queens. It was a coquette of a town, a slender brunette of black eyes and very red lips and cheeks; a Latin brunette of the smoldering, garish type;

a brunette who ran to mantillas and *coquetteries* and very high heels on her glistening slippers. Various times had Mr. Palgrave in his blunt manner compared to Charlotte's disadvantage her alleged beauties with the sedate solidity of his last post, Trebizond in Armenia, whence he had come here to the Caribbean. At first these animadversions of his had been lightly received. Charlotte Amalia was a tolerant lass. This was, perhaps, only a strange variety of British banter! Society had let it go at that; would probably have forgotten all about it. But then the consul-general had made it plain, several times, that he had meant quite literally exactly what he had said. At that Charlotte, though still tolerantly, had been annoyed.

Finally he had been—unconsciously (Charlotte granted that quite definitely)—offensive. He had said certain things. used certain terms, which were—inadvisable. The way he used the word "native," society agreed, was bad diplomacy, to put it mildly. Society continued, because he was a Caucasian and because of his official position, to invite him to its dinners, its routs, its afternoon teas, its swizzel parties. Government House took no notice of his ineptitudes, his comparisons.

The British families, and there were many of these permanently resident in St. Thomas—Chatfields, Talbots, Robertsons, MacDesmonds—were, of course, the backbone of his social relationships. Some of them tried to give him hints when they saw how the wind was veering against him and wishing their own diplomatic representative to be clear of criticism, but these well-intentioned efforts slipped off Mr. Palgrave's uncompromising broad back like water from a duck's!

Then he had really put his foot in it. The leading English magazine to which he was a valued contributor brought out an article by him—on Charlotte Amalia. Here the already famous author of travel articles had commented, in cold print, and disparagingly, upon the society of which he was, for the time being, an integral part. He had, too, been so injudicious as to compare Charlotte Amalia with Trebizond, vastly to the advantage of the Armenian capital. Trebizond, if the man had any sentiment in him, must, at that period, have seemed very attractive in retrospect.

It was chiefly the British West Indians who took in the magazine, but there were a few others. The news of the article spread like wildfire. Extra copies, at Lightbourn's store, were quickly exhausted. Other copies were ordered. Extant copies were worn dog-eared from frequent readings of that *faux pas.* It finished Mr. Palgrave in Charlotte Amalia. A consul-general, and of Great Britain, can hardly be ignored in a comparatively small community. Nevertheless Charlotte Amalia now drew in her perfumed skirts in no unmistakable gesture. There was, of course,

nothing overt about this gesture. Charlotte was far too subtle, far too polite and sophisticated after the Continental manner, for anything crude;
anything, that is, smacking of the consul-general's own methods! But
there was an immediate difference, a delicate, subtle difference, which,
as the weeks progressed, was to make its impact upon the consciousness of William Palgrave, through his thick mental epidermis, in a very
strange manner indeed.

For it had penetrated elsewhere than to the very outer edges of
St. Thomas society. It had got down to Black Quashee himself; down
through the various intervening social strata—minor officials, a few professional persons, shopkeepers, artizans—down to Quashee in his tat-
tered shirt; shoeless, carefree Quashee, at the very bottom of Charlotte
Amalia's social scheme.

Early that spring, at the time when house servants become mysteri-
ously ill and have to be relieved of their duties for a few days, and the
Rata drums, Fad'er, Mama. and Boula de Babee, may be heard to roll
and boom nightly from the wooded hills in the island's interior, and the
Trade Winds' changing direction leaves an almost palpable curtain of
sultriness hanging over the hot, dry town on its three hillsides; in those
days when the burros' tongues hang out of dry mouths along dusty roads
and the centipedes come into the houses out of the dust and street dogs
slink along blazing sidewalks in the narrow slits of house-shade under the broiling sun of late May-time—then, as the Black People came
trickling back into the town from their three or four-day sojourn in the
hills when they make the spring songs—then it was that the Honorable
William Palgrave began to be conscious of a vague, partly realized annoyance, an annoyance which seemed to hang in the air all about him.

As he lay on his handsome carved mahogany bedstead during an
early-afternoon *siesta;* as he sat in his cool shaded office before his great
desk with its dispatch-boxes in orderly rows; as he dressed for dinner
after his late-afternoon bath—taken in the tin tub which he had lugged
about the diplomatic world for the past eighteen years—at such times
the new annoyance would drift to him in whispers, on the dull wings
of the sultry air so hard to breathe for one of his portly habit.It was a
sound-annoyance; a vague, thin, almost imperceptible thing. It was a
tune, with certain elusive words; words of which he heard recurrent bits,
snatches, snippets, incidental mere light touches of a delicate, withering
sarcasm—directed toward him as a child might blow thistledown with
faint derisive intent in the direction of somebody who has managed to
incur its dislike.

The St. Thomas negroes, so it became borne in upon Mr. Palgrave's
understanding, had "made a song on" him.

It was a characteristic, quickstep kind of song; something in the nature of a folksong. Of these there are various examples, like the one wherein the more urban St. Thomian makes fun of his Santa Crucian neighbor by alleging that: "De Crucian gyurl don' wash dey skin," and which ends on the rollicking chorus: "Wash yo'self in a sardine-tin!"

In the course of the weeks in which he was obliged to listen to it, Mr. Palgrave came to recognize the tune, and even a few of the words, which, because of almost incessant repetition, had been forced, though with a delicacy that was almost eery, upon his attention. The tune went to the lilt of the small drum—Boula, de babee—somewhat as follows:

The words, of which there were many, resolved themselves, so far as his appreciation of them was concerned, into two first lines, and a refrain, thus:

"Weelum Palgrave is a Cha-Cha, b'la-hoo!
Him are a koind of a half-a-Jew!"
Then the refrain:
"Him go back to Trebizond."

There were, in these apparently Mother Goose words, various hidden meanings. "B'la-hoo," a contraction from "bally-hoo," is the name of a small, hard-fleshed, surface-water fish, not unlike the flying-fish in consistency, and living, like its winged neighbor, on the surface of deeps. As used in the verses it intensified "Cha-Cha." A Cha-Cha—so-called, it is currently believed in St. Thomas, because of the peculiar sneezing nasality with which these French poor-whites enunciate their Norman French—is one of a peculiarly St. Thomian community, originally emigres from St. Bartholomew's, now so thoroughly inbred as to look all alike—brave and hardy fishermen who can not swim, West Indian poor-whites of the lowest class, like the Barbadian "red-legs." A Cha-Cha B'la-hoo means a particularly Cha Chaish Cha-Cha; an indubitable Cha-Cha. The application of such a term to the consul-general meant that he was of the lowest sort of humanity the St. Thomian negro could name.

Being "half-a-Jew" did not at all mean that Mr. Palgrave partook, as the bearer might easily imagine, of any characteristics believed to inhere in the co-religionists of Moses and Aaron. The phrase had a far deeper—and lower—significance than that The significant portion of it was that word "half." That, stated plainly, meant an aspersion upon the legitimacy of Mr. Palgrave's birth, It was, that epithet, essentially a *"tu quoque"* type of insult—*you're another!* It referred directly to one of Mr. Palgrave's mordant aspersions upon the quality of the St. Thomians, or, rather, upon the class, the negroes, which was now retaliating. It was not the usual custom of these negroes to marry. It had not been their custom in Africa. Their Danish overlords did not compel it here. Why should this foreigner, this Bukra of the double-chin, cast his aspersions upon them? How was he concerned? Not at all, was Black Quashee's obvious reply, according to the logic of the situation. His equally obvious retort, to drum-beats, was:"Him are a koind of a half-a-Jew!"

But—the real gist of the retort, compared to which these glancing blows at his self-esteem were mere thrusts of the *banderillo,* goads-was the refrain:"Him go back to Trebizond."

It was not, precisely, a command. It was still less a statement of accomplished fact. Mr. Palgrave had not gone back to his esteemed Armenian post; Mr. Palgrave had no intention whatever of applying to Downing Street for a transfer back there. It was—a suggestion.

It was that refrain which La Touche Penn had been whistling as he walked demurely away down the glaring white road under the blazing sunlight. Mr. Palgrave stared angrily after the slouching figure; stared after it, an uncompromising scowl upon his handsome, florid features, until it disappeared abruptly around a sudden turn half-way down the hill. Then he mounted the step of his barouche and settled himself in the exact center of the sun-heated leather cushion, a linen dust-cloth over his knees.

It was a Tuesday afternoon, and later, at five o'clock, it was Mr. Palgrave's intention to call at Government House. Governor Arendrup was receiving that afternoon, as he did once a month, but between now and then there was an interval of an hour and a half which the consul-general meant to spend in making duty calls.

Claude, very erect, drove carefully down the hill, turned the sharp corner around which La Touche Penn had disappeared, and thence, by a devious route, descended the slight slope leading to the chief thorough-fare along the sea's edge. Here he turned to the left, passed that mas-sive structure, the Grand Hotel, driving between it and Emancipation Park, turned once more to the left, and soon the wiry little carriage-horses were sweating up one of Charlotte Amalia's steepest hills. They moved carefully around hair-breadth turns guarded by huge clumps of cacti, and at last emerged near the summit of Government Hill. Claude stopped before the entrance to a massive residence perched atop a still higher rise in the land.

Mr. Palgrave climbed steps to the stone and cement terrace of this house and gave to the expressionless black butler his card for Mrs. Talbot. The servant took his stick and hat and led the way up a flight of stairs to Mrs. Talbot's drawing-room. As the consul-general mounted behind his ebony guide he became aware of a tap-tapping, a light sound as though made by the fingers of a supple hand on a kitchen pan. The tapping went: "oóm—bom, bom; oóm—bom, bom; oóm—bom, bom," over and over, monotonously. Accompanying this beat was a light, almost childish, voice; one of the black maids, probably, in some distant portion of the great house. The tune was the tune La Touche Penn had been whistling as he slouched down the hill. Mr. Palgrave mentally supplied the words:

"Weelum Palgrave is a Cha-Cha, b'la-hoo!
Him are a koind of a half-a-Jew—
Him go back to Trebizond!"

It was maddening, this sort of thing. It should not be allowed. Here, in Mrs. Talbot's house! A choleric red disfigured Mr. Palgrave's handsome face as he walked into the drawing-room. It took him several minutes to reassume his accustomed urbanity.

Something Mrs. Talbot said, too, was annoying.

"I am sure I can not say where I acquired the idea, Mr. Palgrave, but—somehow—it came to me that you were not remaining with us; that you were expecting to go back; to Armenia, was it not?"

"I have no such intention—I assure you." Mr. Palgrave felt himself suddenly pink in the face. He used his handkerchief. May, in this climate, is very warm. Mrs. Talbot hoped he would not mind the summer heat.

"We find the sea bathing refreshing," she had vouchsafed.

Mr. Palgrave did not outstay the twenty-minute minimum for a duty call. As he descended the broad stairway he heard the tap-tapping once more, but now the words accompanying it were muted. There was no song. He found himself repeating the doggerel words to the tapping of that damnable pan:

"Him go back to Trebizond."

Absurd! He should do nothing of the sort. Only fancy—blackamoors! To suggest such a thing—to him! He descended the steps to the roadway a picture of complacent dignity.

A tiny barefooted black child strolled past, an empty kerosene-tin balanced on her kinky, kerchiefed head. The child, preoccupied with a wilted bougainvillea blossom which she held between her hands, hummed softly, a mere tuneless little murmur, barely audible on the freshening Trade Wind of mid-afternoon. Mr. Palgrave, his perceptions singularly sensitive this afternoon, caught it, however. His directions for the next call were given to black Claude almost savagely.

Precisely at five he mounted the steps of Government House. He was saluted in form by the pair of Danish *gendarmes,* in their stiff Frederick the Great uniforms, from each side of the doorway. He subscribed his name and titles in the visitors' book. He gave up his hat and stick to another saluting *gendarme,* and mounted the interior stairway to the great drawing-room above.Here all St. Thomas society congregated monthly at the governor's reception, and with those who had arrived on time this afternoon the drawing-room was half filled. The Governor's Band, outside on the east end of the iron gallery which runs along the front of Government House, started up an air. Officers, officials, the clergy, the town's gentry, the other resident consuls, and the ladyfolk of all these, passed solemnly in review before the governor, stiff in his black clothes, shaking hands formally in his box-like frock coat, his spotless white kid gloves.

Mr. Palgrave, still ruffled from his afternoon's experiences, greeted His Danish Majesty's representative in this loyal colony with a stiffness quite equal to the governor's, and passed within. Ladies seated at both ends of a vast mahogany table in the dining-room dispensed coffee and tea. Mounded along the table's sides stood great silver trays of "spread," half-sandwiches of white and brown bread covered with cheese, with preserves, with ground meats, with *liver-pastei.* At the sideboard Santa Cruz rum, made in the colony, French brandy imported from Martinique, and Danish beer in small bottles and served with fine pieces of ice in the glasses, were being rapidly dispensed by liveried negro servants to a crowd which stood eight deep.From this group a burly figure, that of Captain the Honorable William McMillin, detached itself and accosted Mr. Palgrave. The captain, administrator of Great Fountain Estate over on Santa Cruz, here for the day on some estate business for his kinsmen the Comyns family who all lived in Scotland and for whom he managed their Santa Crucian sugar interests, had been as a freshly commissioned Cornet of Horse, one of Wellington's officers more than fifty years before, at Waterloo. The old gentleman invited Mr. Palgrave to a bottle of the Carlsburg beer, and the two Britons, provided with this refreshing beverage, sat down to talk together.

In their armchairs the two made a notable appearance, both being large-bodied, florid men, and the aged captain wearing, as was his custom on state occasions, his ancient scarlet military coat. Outside the great open French windows, the band members on the gallery, between pieces, made themselves heard as they arranged their music. Save for the bandmaster, Erasmus Petersen, a Dane, all were negroes. Through the windows came minor musical sounds as a slide was shifted in an alto horn or as little runs and flutings tested the precision of a new tuning. In the midst of this, delicately, almost incidentally, the oboist ran his swart fingers over his silver keys, breathed into his instrument. A rippling, muted little quickstep came through the windows:

"Weelum Palgrave is a Cha-Cha, b'la-hoo!"

Mr. Palgrave suddenly shifted in his armchair. Then he remembered that he could not appear to notice this deliberate slap in the face, and, though suddenly empurpled, he sat quiet. He collected his wits, invited the captain to dinner that evening, and excused himself.

Claude, attentive for once, noted his emergence below, extricated his barouche, reached the steps where the two wooden-soldierlikeg-endarmes were saluting his master."Home!" said Mr. Palgrave, acidly, stepping into the carriage.

That evening Mr. Palgrave opened his grief to his fellow Briton, as to a person of assured position and integrity, the consul-general's face quite purple between his vexation and the bottle of sound burgundy he had consumed at dinner.

The captain took his consul-general's annoyance lightly.

"Man, man!" he expostulated, "ye're no so clearly accustomed to 'Quashee' and his ways as mysel,' I do assure you. Why—there's a song about me! My field-hands made it up, years ago. It runs:

'Mars' McMillin la' fo' me,
Loike him la' to Waterloo!'

"And it means that I command them—that is to 'la,' Mr. Palgrave— the same as I gave commands at Waterloo— there were a-precious few, I do assure you, sir. I was no more than a cornet at the time, my commission not two weeks old." The captain proceeded to pooh-pooh the Quashee songs as reason for serious annoyance.

But his explanations left Mr. Palgrave cold.

"Your negroes do not—er—*insist* upon your returning to the Low Countries to fight Waterloo all over again!" was his bitter comment. That suggestion that he return to Trebizond had bitten deep.He had Trebizond on his mind when he was retiring that night and it is not strange that he went back there where he had spent two profitable years before being assigned to Charlotte Amalia, in his dreams. Somehow, as the strange distortion of the dream-state provides, he was identified with the sage Firdûsi, a great hero of Armenian legend, that same Firdûsi who had defied a Shah of Persia and refused to compose a history of his life at the imperial command.

Identified with Firdûsi, of whom he had heard many tales, Mr. Palgrave suffered imprisonment in his dreams; was, like Firdûsi, summoned again and again into the Presence, always with refusal on his lips; always to be sent back to a place of confinement of increasing comfortlessness.

At last Palgrave-Firdûsi returned to an empty cell where for days he sat on the earthen floor, refusing to yield, to stultify himself. Then, on a gray morning, his jailer entered leading a blind slobbering negro who sat on the floor opposite him. For an interminable period he suffered this disagreeable companionship. The Black was dumb as well as blind. He sat there, day after day, night after night, cross-legged on the hard floor.

At last Palgrave-Firdûsi could stand it no longer. He howled for his jailer, demanded audience. He was led to the throne room, his resolution dissipated, his one overwhelming desire to acquiesce—yes, yes; he would write—only let him be free of that slobbering horror which mewed to itself with its blank slab of a mouth. He threw himself face down before the throne.

The impact of his prostration awakened him, shivering, in his great mahogany bed. The moonlight of the Caribes poured through the opened jalousies of the airy bedroom high on the hillsides of Charlotte Amalia: and through the open windows came eerily—it was three o'clock in the morning—the very ghost of a little lilting refrain in the cracked voice of some aged man:

"Him go back-to Trebizond."

Mr. Palgrave groaned, roiled over in bed so that his better ear was undermost, sought to woo sleep again.

But now it was impossible to sleep. That tune—that devilish, that damnable tune-was running through his head again, tumultuously, to the small-drum throbbing of his heart. He groaned and tossed impatiently, miserably. Would morning never come?

In a gray dawn Mr. Palgrave rose from an unrefreshing bed, tubbed himself half-heartedly. His face, as he looked at it in his shaving-mirror, wielding his Wednesday Wade & Butcher, seemed gray and drawn; there was no color in his usually choleric cheeks. The servants, at this hour, would not have arrived. There would be no morning tea ready.

At a little before seven, fully dressed, Mr. Palgrave descended the staircase to his office below. He sat down at his orderly desk, listening to the shuffle of early-morning bare feet outside there on the earthen hillside roadway before his fine house; to the clipped, grave snatches of the creole speech of the Blacks; to the occasional guffaws of the negroes about their early-morning occasions; gravely erect; carrying trays, fruits, great tins of cistern-water, atop kerchiefed heads.

Mechanically he reached for his writing-materials, dipped a pen in an inkwell, commenced to write. He wrote on and on, composing carefully, the edge of his mind engaged in listening for the song out there on the roadway. He discovered that he was tapping out its cadence with his foot on the scrubbed pitch-pine flooring underneath his desk: oóm—bom, bom; oóm—bom, bom; oóm—bom, bom; oóm-bom, bom!

He finished his letter, signed it meticulously, blotted it, folded it twice, then heard the latch of the remote kitchen door snap. He rose, walked into the dining-room, and spoke through the inner kitchen door to Melissa his cook who had just arrived:

"Make me some tea at once, if you please."

"Yes, sar." It was the dutiful, monotonous, unhurried voice of old Black Melissa as she motivated herself ponderously in the direction of the charcoal barrel in the kitchen's corner.

Mr. Palgrave reflectively mounted the stairs to his bedroom. He was putting a keen edge on his Wednesday razor—he used a set of seven—before it dawned upon him that he had already shaved! He returned the razor to its case. What could be the matter with him? He looked musingly into his shaving-mirror, passed a well-kept hand reflectively over the smooth cheeks into which the exercise of moving about and up and down the stairs had driven a little of his accustomed high color. He shook his head at his reflection in the glass, walked out into the upper hallway, redescended the stairs, once more entered his office.

What was this?

He frowned, stared, picked up from the desk the letter he had finished ten minutes before, examined it carefully. It was, unquestionably, in his own handwriting. The ink was barely dry. He laid it back in its place on the desk and began to pace the room, slowly, listening to Melissa's slow movings-about in the kitchen, to the arrival of other servants. He could hear their clipped greetings to the old cook.

Wondering at himself, at this strange mental world where he found himself, he seated himself firmly, judicially, in his ample desk chair, picked up the letter, read it through again with an ever-increasing wonderment. He laid it down, his thoughts turning, strangely to Trebizond.

And Mr. Palgrave could not, for the life of him, recall writing this letter.

He was still sitting there, staring blankly at nothing, his brows drawn together in a deep frown, when Claude came in to announce tea prepared in the dining-room. "Tea," in St. Thomas, Continental fashion, is the name of the morning meal. "Breakfast" comes at one o'clock. Mr. Palgrave's cook had prepared amply that morning, but not bacon and eggs, nor even Scotch marmalade, availed to arouse him from his strange preoccupation.

After "tea" he sat again at his desk alone until ten o'clock, when his privacy was invaded by two sailors from a British vessel in the harbor, with consular business to transact. He gave these men his careful attention; later, his advice. He walked out with them an hour later, turned up the hill and strolled about the steep hillside streets for an hour.

It was nearly high noon when he returned. He passed the office, going upstairs to refresh his appearance after his walk. It was blistering hot outdoors under the May noon sunlight drenching the dusty roadways.

When he went into his office half an hour later he saw the letter once more. It was enclosed now, in an official envelope, addressed, too, in his own unmistakable handwriting, duly stamped for posting. Again, he had no slightest recollection of having done any of these things. He picked up the letter intending now to tear it across and then across again and fling the bits of paper into the waste-basket. Instead he sat with it in his hands, curiously placid, in an apathetic state in which he seemed not even to think. He ended by placing it in his coat pocket and was immediately afterward summoned to the one o'clock "breakfast" in the dining-room.

When he awakened from his siesta that afternoon it was near four o'clock. He remembered the letter at once. He rose, and before his afternoon bath examined the coat pocket. The letter was not in the pocket. He decided to look for it on the desk later.

In half an hour, fresh and cool now after his bath, he descended the stairway and went straight into his office. The letter was on his mind, and, frowning slightly, he stepped toward the immaculately neat desk. He drew down his lip under his teeth in a puzzled expression. The letter was not on the desk.

The arrival of callers summoned him into the drawing-room. He did not give any thought to the letter again until dinner-time and then he was at the top of Government Hill at one of the British houses and could only postpone his desire to find and destroy it.

The letter failed to turn up, and the next day came and passed, and the next after it, and the days stretched into weeks. He had almost forgotten the letter. It cropped up mentally now and then as a vague, half-remembered annoyance. Things were going better these days. The song and its varied accompaniments of drum-tapping, whistling, humming of the nearly soundless tune, the encompassing annoyance, it had caused him—all these things seemed to have dropped out of the hearing, and consequently out of the mind of the consul-general. He felt, as he half realized, somewhat more at home now in Charlotte Amalia. Everybody, it appeared, was perfectly courteous to him. The atmosphere of vague hostility which had vaguely adumbrated his surroundings was gone, utterly dissipated. The charm of the town had begun to appeal to this sophisticated traveler of the earth's surfaces.

Then one morning among the letters which the Royal Mail steamer *Hyperion* had brought into the harbor the night before he discerned an official communication from his superiors in London.He opened it before any of his other letters, as was natural.

The Under-Secretary had written granting his urgent request to be sent back to Trebizond. He was requested to take immediate passage to any convenient Mediterranean port and to proceed thence direct to the Armenian capital. It was, at the moment, agreeable to the consular service that he should be there. Suggestions followed in the letter's text, designating various policies to be pursued.

He finished the many sheets of thin onion-skin paper, folded the letter and laid it on the desk, and sat, staring dully at his inkwell. He did not want to go back to Trebizond. He wanted to remain here. But—he had no choice in the matter. He cudgeled his brains warily. He recalled his singular apathy at the time when his letter—written, it seemed, as though subconsciously—had disappeared. He had not *wanted*to write that letter. He recalled that there had been confusion in his mind at the time—he could not, he recalled, remember the actual writing, nor sending it after it was written. There was something very strange here, something—unusual! Indubitably he had applied for transfer to Trebizond. To Trebizond he was ordered to go!Charlotte Amalia, that coy Latin-brunette of a town with her *coquetteries* and her too-garish coloring, and her delicate beauties—Charlotte Amalia had schemed for his departure, forced his hand, driven him out. He sat there, at his desk, thinking, ruefully, of many things. Then his pride came to his rescue. He remembered the slights which had been put upon him, those intangible slights—the almost formless little tune with its absurd, gibberish words; the tapping of pans; the rattle and boom of the hill drums, those detestable night drums on which these stupid-looking, subtle blackamoors were always and forever, and compellingly, tapping, tapping, tapping.And before very long Mr. Palgrave, who did not believe in magic and who pooh-poohed anything labeled "eery" or "occult" as absurd; who believed only in unmistakable matters like sound beef and County Families and exercise and the integrity of the British Empire and the invariable inferiority of foreigners—Mr. Palgrave came to see that in some fashion not accounted for in his philosophy Charlotte Amalia had played him a very scurvy trick-somehow.

Bestirring himself he began to examine the inventory which he kept of his household gear; many belongings without which no British gentleman could be expected to exist. He indited to the harbor-master a cold, polite note, requesting notice of the arrival of vessels clearing for Mediterranean ports or ports on the Black Sea—Odessa for choice—and he began to formulate, in his small, precise handwriting, the list of duty-calls which must be made before his departure. In the pauses between these labors he wrote various polite, stiff notes, and in the very midst of such activities Claude summoned him to midday breakfast.

Leading the way to the dining-room after this announcement, Claude paused at the office doorway, turned a deprecating face to his employer.

"Yes?" said Mr. Palgrave, perceiving that Claude wished to address him.

"Yo' is leave us, sar," said Claude, with courteous absence of any inflection or emphasis on his words which would indicate that he was asking a question.

"Yes—I am leaving very shortly," replied Mr. Palgrave unemotion-ally. He added nothing to this statement. He was a stiff master to his servants, just but distant. Servants had their place and must be kept in it, according to Mr. Palgrave's scheme of life.

That night, his sleep being rather fitful, Mr. Palgrave noted that the drums were reiterating some message, insistently, up in the hills.

Neither Claude, who as coachman-butler had the closest contact with his employer of any of the house servants, nor, indeed, old Melissa nor any of the others, made any further remark to their employer concerning his departure. This took place three days later, on a Netherlands vessel clearing for Genoa; and Mr. Palgrave was probably the very last person in St. Thomas who would have asked any personal question of a servant.

Yet he wondered, when it occurred to him—and that was often—just how Claude had known he was leaving.

Made in the USA
Middletown, DE
26 December 2023

46757605R00090